TWO COWBOYS SAVE CHRISTMAS

LACEY DAVIS

VIRTUAL BOOKSELLER

Can Christmas Be Saved

Orphaned as a child, twenty-year-old Christmas Rawls only wants a real family and loving husband. Ripped from the orphanage, she is sold to a whorehouse by the corrupt orphanage director where she realizes she's not the first to be victimized.

Noel Brooks and August Hamilton are lonely cowboys with nothing but a ranch that needs a woman's touch. On a trip to Blessing, Texas, they see a terrified woman whose innocence touches them. Instead of buying cattle, they purchase the woman. Saving her is the plan, but in doing so, they throw all of them into more danger than they can handle alone.

Determined to stop the nefarious director, can Christmas save the children or will she be silenced for eternity? Can two cowboys, who are forever transformed, save Christmas?

Sign up for my New Book Alert and receive a complimentary book — Blindfold Me.

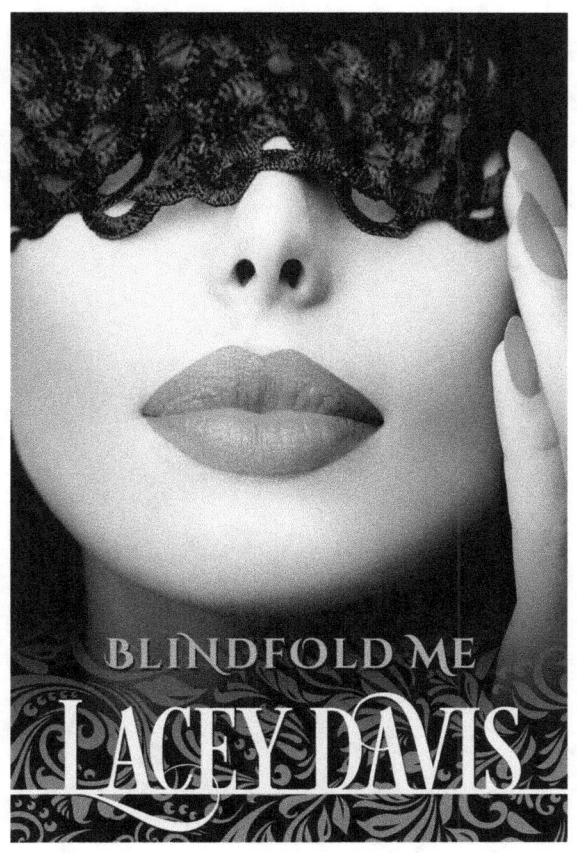

https://www.subscribepage.com/laceydavis_author

CHAPTER 1

Christmas Rawls loved helping the children of the orphanage decorate the cedar tree for the holiday. Unless the women in town brought the children presents, there would be nothing under the tree. Such was the life of an orphan.

Outside, the cold wind rattled the windows in the old house, seeping inside. She would need to bundle the little ones tightly to keep them warm tonight in the drafty rooms.

"Jennifer, can you put the paper star on the top?"

The girl reached up and tied it onto the tree, where it promptly fell over.

"Let me do it," David said. The boy moved the hand-cut design farther down the stem, and then with a bow, managed to keep the star on top. At thirteen, he would soon be leaving to find his way on his own.

Christmas stared at each of the children. Each had arrived in their own special way. Each held a special place in her heart. Christmas hated the idea of having to leave; she loved the children and took care of them. They were her family. They made her happy.

On Christmas day, she would turn twenty. She knew it was time to go, but this was the only home she'd ever known. As a toddler, she'd been left on the doorstep on Christmas Eve, and the lady who ran the orphanage named her Christmas.

Mrs. Griffin had long since died, and now the place was run by Mr. Stephens, who cut corners and tried to make the place profitable, but with ten mouths ranging in age from two to twenty, it was difficult.

One of the smaller kids, Benjamin, jumped up and down, happily. "Santa?"

"That's right, Santa will arrive in one week," she told them.

At her age, she was accustomed to not receiving gifts, but for the sake of the children, she hoped the town would remember them during this special time of year.

The orphanage sat on the outskirts of the town of Blessing and most of the time, the people were generous to help them.

The babies were adopted, but the older children usually remained until they left on their own. She was the eldest there; those older had already gone into the world. Some in the middle of the night. Those were the troubling ones. Especially the young women. Where had they gone? Why hadn't they said good-bye?

Mr. Stephens walked out of his office and stared at their makeshift tree. "Time for bed."

Turning, she glanced at the man whose presence she avoided. When he gazed at her, it was like he undressed her with his eyes, and the thought made her shiver with revulsion.

2

There was something about him that had her intuition warning her to stay far away.

"Come, children, and I'll tuck you in."

As the seven little ones and three older children climbed the groaning stairs under where the roof leaked, she couldn't help but think of this place as home. It was all she knew, and yet if repairs were not soon made, the place would fall down around their ears.

With a shiver, she helped the toddlers change into sleeping clothes. This was her favorite time of night. When she put the little ones to bed, read to the older children, then ushered them into the main room where they all slept.

After everyone was settled in for the night, she undressed and crawled into bed. She turned down the lantern to where she could read from the latest book she borrowed from those donated to the home. Here, she could disappear into a story and not worry about her future.

Mr. Stephens opened the door. "Christmas, I need to see you."

"Yes, sir," she said as she waited for him to close the door before she rose from the bed.

"What do you think he wants?" Jennifer asked her. At fourteen, the girl was often anxious. She worried about everything. She had yet to realize that they didn't have much control over their lives at this time.

"Oh, probably one of the little ones is sick. You know he doesn't like to care for them when they're ill."

The man didn't seem to like children and it was one of the reasons she stayed. Who would care for them if she weren't here?

Crawling out of bed, she picked up her wrapper and put it

around herself. He had never entered the room this late at night and a trickle of unease wound itself around her middle.

Whatever could he want?

Before she went downstairs, she checked on the toddlers. They were fast asleep. Nervous flutters settled in her stomach as she hurried down the creaking stairs.

When she stepped into his office, two men jumped from behind the door. They were rough looking and hadn't seen a razor or a bath in a long time.

"She'll do," the man said as he shoved a bandana between her lips.

"Told you she was a beauty," Mr. Stephens said.

Fear sparkled down her spine and she struggled to get away, but her hands were being pulled behind her back and tied. The other man placed a tow sack over her head, engulfing her in darkness.

"Damn shame to hide all this beauty. But where you're going, it will make you lots of money."

What in the hell was he referring to?

She screamed, but only garbled sounds came from between her lips.

"Here's the cash," she heard the man say.

"Tell the madam she owes me a free sample," Mr. Stephens said.

Dear God, Mr. Stephens was selling her. But to whom? Madam who?

Hands wrapped around her upper arms, and they dragged her from the room and out the door of the house. The cold night air seeped beneath her bed clothes. All she wore was her nightgown, wrapper, and bloomers. She began to fight in earnest, knowing that once they put her in that wagon, she would never return to the orphanage.

"Stop fighting," the man said. "Don't make me hurt you."

Tears trickled down her face. Not even a chance to say good-bye to the children. Who would take care of them?

She felt herself lifted into a wagon and then they were riding away from the only home she had ever known.

CHAPTER 2

*S*itting at the bar in the bordello, Noel Brooks took a sip of his whiskey and tried to ignore his friend August Hamilton.

Glancing around the crowded establishment, he noted more men here tonight than they had ever seen. More men, fewer ladies.

"You promised me on this trip that we could hire a hooker. Here we are in the whorehouse and you're sitting there sipping whiskey like we have all night."

His friend was getting impatient with him, but Noel had not seen a woman he couldn't live without.

It was true, Noel had promised August that they would share a woman tonight, but something was holding him back. It was damn near Christmas, the time of year he hated.

Maybe it would be good for him to have a woman suck his cock, but he'd rather drown himself in a whiskey bottle and pray that the alcohol dulled all the feelings and emotions.

Almost twenty years later, he still remembered the dark-haired girl falling into the river. His best friend Sadie Jones.

He'd battled the water to reach her but failed. And every year, he remembered that sweet face.

Every year, he remembered her and thought about what would have happened if she hadn't died. Because he had such a huge crush on her.

But he had promised August and his word was gold.

"As soon as I finish my whiskey, we can start looking," he said, wanting to put it off for as long as possible. Not because he didn't think a woman would be good for him, but rather, he just wasn't in the mood.

They were in town to buy cattle for next year's herd and even that didn't thrill him. Their ranch was doing very well, but it needed a woman. It needed the sound of laughter and children's squeals as they ran outside.

"Don't get too excited," August said with sarcasm. "It's not like we were here last week. It's been months and my cock is hard as granite."

"Your cock stays hard," Noel said as he took another sip and finished off the drink. One more whiskey to wash the pain away.

Though they lived not far out of town, they spent their time working to make their ranch a successful operation. Their focus for the last several years had been building a barn, a bunkhouse, and a home. Their herd was growing, but it was time to introduce new blood. And thus, their reason for coming into Blessing.

"Don't you dare order another one," August said.

Suddenly, loud cheering came from the room next door.

"What's going on in there?" August asked the bartender, curious about the noise.

"They're auctioning off the newest girl, a virgin," he said.

7

The clamor drew Noel and he stood and walked into the room. August was at his side as they entered where a young woman stood on a table in a white lace dress. Dark hair framed her innocent pale face and terrified emerald eyes. "This young woman arrived yesterday, and tonight we're holding an auction. If you want to be the first man to claim her virginity, the bidding is about to begin."

"How do we know she's a virgin?" a man screamed.

The madam smiled and pointed to a man in the corner.

"She's a virgin," the man said. "I'm a doctor and her hymen is intact."

Tears rolled down the woman's face and the madam came up behind her and slapped her on the ass. "Stop sniffling and smile to the crowd."

Though the woman's full bottom lip trembled, she did her best to smile and he wondered how many times she'd been beaten since she arrived at the whorehouse.

"Now, who will be the first to bid?" The woman in a fine silk dress turned and smiled at the men in the crowd. "You could be her first, but not her last."

The woman laughed at her joke and a trickle of anger spiraled through Noel. Did the madam have no decency? The young girl was barely more than a child. And she looked like Sadie.

"Five dollars," a man called out.

The madam acted outraged. "She's a virgin. No man has ever touched her and you'd be the one training her. You can do better than that or I'll send her back to the farm."

"Ten," another man said.

Like a Texas tornado, Noel's anger gripped him and he

leaned down to speak to August. "She's terrified. She's hurting. I can't watch this. We've got to save her."

August glared at him like he was crazy. "How much are you going to offer?"

"Two hundred," Noel said.

"That's our cattle buying money," August said in shock. "Plus, you promised me a woman tonight."

Noel gazed at the woman who was smiling though tears streamed down her cheeks. What if that was Sadie? Or even one of his sisters? How could he watch her be auctioned off to one of these randy, rowdy cowboys? It wasn't possible.

Though he knew August didn't approve, he couldn't stop himself.

He held up his hand. "One hundred dollars."

A gasp went around the room and the madam glanced out and smiled at him. "Now, that's more like it."

Another man upped his bid and when they got to one hundred and fifty, Noel raised his hand. "Two hundred dollars."

There was silence in the room.

The madam began to speak. "Going once, going twice, sold to the gentleman in the back."

A burly man approached them. "Come with me."

They were led into the back of the brothel to a cashier.

"Two hundred," the man said to an older woman sitting behind a cage.

Noel pulled out his billfold and handed the woman two one-hundred-dollar bills.

"I hope like hell you know what you're doing," August said in a low whisper.

The man smiled at them. "She'll be waiting in room two for you. It's her first time, so be gentle, but make certain she learns to be a good fuck. After all, she'll be working again later tonight." A chill spiraled through Noel. Why he thought they were getting her alone for the entire night, he didn't know, but obviously they were going to make her work after them. By purchasing her virginity, they weren't saving her. They were merely postponing the inevitable fact that she was going to be a whore if she remained here.

As they followed a woman up the stairs, all he could think about was how they could help her escape.

"I don't know what you're thinking, but this can't be good," August said softly. "We should have just hired an experienced girl and left."

"Shut up, August," he hissed, hoping the woman in front of him hadn't heard anything his friend said.

The stairs were narrow as they climbed to the second floor. As they passed rooms, grunts and groans and even a few moans were heard. The thought of his sisters or Sadie having to work in such a place had his insides tense.

The woman stopped in front of room two. She checked to make certain the girl was in the room and then she smiled at them. "Enjoy, gentlemen. You have one hour."

For two hundred dollars, they only had one hour? The madam was making a lot of money on this girl tonight.

They walked through the door and the madam pulled it shut behind them. Noel reached over and flipped the lock.

The woman lay tied to the bed, naked. Full soft breasts gave way to a small waist, rounded hips, and legs that were long enough to wrap around a man's waist as he drove his cock into her sweet pussy.

For a moment, they stopped and stared at her beautiful curves. Dark hair lay against the pillow as her emerald eyes gazed at them with horror.

"Dear God, maybe you weren't a fool after all," August said as he stared at her.

"No, we're going to save her," Noel said as he walked to her.

Her eyes grew wide and he could see fear filled them. Never had he ever wanted to see terror in a woman's eyes again. The memory of Sadie struggling to reach him engulfed and terrorized him. He took a deep breath to calm the raging emotions inside him.

"I'm not going to hurt you," he said as he sank down on the bed and began to loosen her ties.

"What are you doing?" August said. "Let's take advantage. My cock is near bursting."

"No," Noel said, knowing he could never take a woman like this. "We're rescuing her. Go relieve yourself if you must, but you're not touching this woman."

His friend shook his head and sighed. "You've got that damn stubborn look. There's no changing your mind, is there?"

The woman had stopped crying and stared at them in confusion. She licked her lips and watched as Noel continued to untie her from the bed.

"You're not going to rape me?"

"No, we're going to try to help you. Get dressed," Noel said as August began to work on the ties that held her feet to the posts.

"Wait a minute," August said, gazing at her. "Did you agree to this?"

The woman's eyes widened. "Of courses not. They kidnapped me."

"What's your name, darling," Noel asked.

"Christmas," she whispered.

The two men exchanged glances.

"Really?"

"Yes," she said.

"Well, don't that just beat all," August said, smiling. "We were going to fuck Christmas. I'm August and this is my friend Noel."

Noel shook his head and walked over to the to the window and glanced down.

"All I wanted was a simple night with a woman sucking my cock and plunging into her sweet pussy, and instead, I'm mixed up trying to rescue a woman named Christmas from a whorehouse. What the hell?" August said, shaking his head. "Noel, you're really fucking this up."

"Shut up and help me. We're on the side of the building. Our horses are tied out in front."

"You got anything else besides that skimpy dress?" August asked her, looking about the room.

She jumped up from the bed and ran to where her clothes were piled on a chair. It was a damn shame to cover all that beauty, but if they were not going to be killed, they needed to get out of here before the madam told them time was up.

"No," she said softly as she was putting the horrid dress back on. No, it wasn't terrible, just a little piece of silk that barely covered her delights and clung to her like a second skin.

She glanced between the two men, nervous.

"Noel is trying to figure out a way to get you out of here without us all getting killed."

Noel noticed the window was nailed shut. A scowl crossed his face. Someone else had tried to escape from the whorehouse and he wondered at the number of women who could be working here against their will.

He pulled out his pocketknife and pried the nails out. Soon the window lifted and he motioned the two of them over.

"This is not going to be easy. I'm going to slide down the metal roof and then drop down to the ground. Christmas on my signal, you go next and I'll do my best to catch you. August, you come down last."

"We've got to be prepared to leave in a hurry, so once we reach the horses, we ride."

August shook his head. "Damn, man, you know how to ruin a good time."

His friend was often a whiner and complainer, but Noel ignored the man.

"We're saving Christmas. It's going to be just fine," Noel said as he crawled out the window. He grunted when hitting the ground and then gave a whistle.

His biggest fear was that she would scream, but the woman didn't make a sound as she slid down the slick metal roof. Until he caught her in his arms.

"Oh, my," she said calmly.

The feel of her soft body sliding down his was enough to make his dick pound with want, but there was no time for anything but saving her.

Next, came August who laughed when he landed on the ground. "That was a fun ride."

While he waited with Christmas, August went to the front

of the whorehouse and brought their horses around to them. Noel helped Christmas into his saddle.

A woman's voice floated on the air from the entrance. "Mr. Stephens. How nice to see you." The bastard himself stepped up the front stairs.

Christmas tensed in his arms. "Oh no, we've got to go."

Not one to ask questions when he could hear the fear in her voice, he kicked the sides of his mare and dashed down the road away from the place of sin.

A feeling of warmth filled him. Tonight they saved Christmas, but now what did they do?

CHAPTER 3

*C*hristmas had nowhere to go. She could not return to the orphanage. She had no friends or family in the city to whom she could turn to for help. She was all alone.

"Where can we take you?"

"I don't know," she said. "I don't have anyone."

In the darkness, she could see that Noel didn't understand and August, the man who wanted to take her and make her into a whore, was frowning. He seemed like a bully and yet she liked Noel. He was an honest man who had risked his life to save hers.

"What do you mean you don't have anyone?" August asked, his voice rising with frustration. "Didn't the madam threaten to send you back to some farm?"

"Yes, she did, but I didn't come from a farm. I have no one," she said, the feelings of abandonment overwhelming her.

"You're lying," he said.

His pants could get all twisted because, frankly, she didn't care. "I was living at the orphanage when the director sold me to the whorehouse."

Noel's arms around her tensed and she could tell he was upset. August didn't say a word.

"We're going to stay at the hotel tonight. You're welcome to stay with us, but we must sneak you in or otherwise the madam and her henchmen will take you away."

What was she going to do? No place in the town where she had grown up would be safe. While tonight she had a shelter, what would tomorrow bring? Was she just delaying the inevitable?

"Think about it and let me know what you want to do. You're free to leave at any time. We don't expect anything in return," Noel said.

She liked this man. He made her feel safe, like he wanted to protect her and help her, but also there were no stipulations for his assistance.

What would she do? Women like her had nothing and the madam would make certain she could not get a decent job in the town of Blessing. If she went to another town, who would hire her and what were the odds of her finding herself working in a whorehouse again? Only this time, there would be no one to save her.

No, she needed a husband. But who would marry a girl with no good background rescued from a whorehouse? Men didn't consider her a catch. No man had ever even talked of courting her. The only person she knew in town was the pastor and his wife.

She bit her lip. As they rode through the back alleys of Blessing, she knew she needed to ask Noel to marry her. But even that, she felt uncertain about. He'd been kind to her, but he owed her nothing in return.

"Can I spend tonight with you in your hotel room," she said softly.

"Of course," Noel said.

August groaned. "I'm not going to get my Christmas pussy, am I?"

Noel shook his head in the darkness. "Shut up, August," he said. "Christmas doesn't want to hear your complaints."

When they reached the hotel, Noel swung his leg over the horse and helped her from the saddle. August jumped down off his mare. The man frowned at Noel and she could see he didn't like her.

"I'll take care of the horses. You get her in the room without being seen."

Noel took his coat and scarf and arranged it to where all anyone could see were her eyes. The jacket smelled like the man and a pleasant warmth filled her.

"You don't look like a man, but no one can see your face."

He hurried her through the back door of the hotel and as they rounded a corner to go up the stairs, the clerk stopped him. The man's eyes were roaming over Christmas and she tried to make herself as inconspicuous as possible.

"Mr. Brooks, the cattle buyer left you this message," he said, handing him a note and gazed at Christmas with interest.

"Thank you," he said and hurried her up the stairs. "Damn, he saw you. They're going to put a bounty on your head. Whoever turns you in will receive a reward as long as it leads to your capture."

Fear spiraled through her and she had to squeeze her eyes shut to keep the tears at bay. She was in danger with no place to hide or get away. And now she was endangering the men who helped her.

Her situation felt hopeless.

When they walked into the hotel room, Noel lit a lantern as she gazed at the two big beds. Who was sleeping where? With a start, she realized she'd never slept in a hotel before. Noel walked over to the window and glanced outside. The streets were active as wagons rolled down main street.

"The madam is not going to give you up easily. She would make too much money on you."

The thought of how angry she would be filled Christmas with fear. There was no way she could ever go back. Not without facing punishment.

She didn't want to think about returning there tonight.

"I'll take the settee," she said, needing to know their sleeping arrangements, ignoring his comments about Madam Leake.

Noel promised her they would require nothing in return, but she couldn't trust anyone.

"No, you'll sleep in the bed," he told her. "It won't hurt for me to sleep on that couch for one night."

But she wanted and needed more than one night or feared she would find herself back in the bordello. Today, they had kept her away from most of the women working there and she feared that was so she would not understand what was happening until it was too late.

Glancing around the room, she realized there was not a separate bathing area. They were stuck here together, sleeping in the same room. Not even the boys in the orphanage and her had to share the same room.

She unwrapped the scarf from around her face and

removed his coat. She didn't even have more than this dress that was meant to tempt men into bidding on her. The silk fabric left her shoulders bare, fitted her breasts and hung down to the floor with a slit all the way up that revealed her leg.

No wonder the boy at the front desk had been admiring her outfit. And now he knew that a woman wearing a skimpy dress was in Noel's room.

"I'm endangering you," she said. "I should leave."

"No," Noel said. "August and I are capable of protecting ourselves and you."

She sank down on the settee and the dress moved up exposing her leg all the way to the V between her legs. She wore no pantaloons because they would have been exposed.

"Are you hungry?"

It was well past midnight and she had not been given anything to eat since lunch, but her nerves were so tightly strung that she couldn't eat a thing right now.

"No, thank you," she said.

Just then, August walked in. "There was a big commotion out in the street. I think they're starting to search for you."

Noel shook his head. "The desk clerk stopped me on the way up the stairs. He saw her."

Nerves gripped Christmas's stomach. "Maybe I should go."

"You'd be caught within five minutes. Besides, where would you go?"

She had no idea, but the thought of returning to the whorehouse terrified her. And she had worried about the children at the orphanage all day. Who was taking care of them? Certainly not Mr. Stephens.

The man was the devil himself.

Her hands covered her face and she leaned forward on her knees. "I need a husband. Someone I could depend on, who would protect me. Someone..." Tears rolled down her cheeks and she sobbed. "I don't want to be a whore."

Suddenly she felt the settee give as first one man and then the other sat beside her. Noel took her into his arms and August wrapped his arm around her back. A sense of security surrounded her and she gave a little hiccup.

"Oh, darling, we'll do our best to keep you safe," Noel said.

"Don't worry, we're not going to take you back or let them have you," August said. "You're safe with us."

And she appreciated that, but she couldn't stay with them forever. Sooner or later, she had to make it on her own.

"Are you serious about looking for a husband," Noel said.

What where her options? She was alone in this world, without food, money, or even clothes. What choice did she have except to return to the whorehouse where she knew the madam would punish her for running away.

And punishment from the madam was severe, painful, and left marks.

"Noel," August said in a low tone.

The man did not like her. She didn't know why or what she had done to him or maybe that's how he felt about all women. She didn't know that much about men, her only experience had been with Mr. Stephens and she hated him.

"Excuse us for a minute, Christmas," Noel said. "We need to speak privately."

The two men removed their arms from around her, stood, and walked into the hallway. Still on the couch, she could hear their raised voices and knew August was protesting something.

The door opened and the two men walked in together.

They sat beside her and she could see that Noel was nervous and August frustrated.

"Christmas, we're best of friends. At times we disagree, but since we moved not far from Blessing, we've chosen a different kind of life. The only reason we were at the whorehouse tonight was to share a woman between us."

What? Men did such a thing? A shiver went through her at the thought of everything she would have been forced to do working there.

"Oh," she said, not really understanding.

August picked up her hand. "You're an innocent. We like to make love to a woman at the same time. We share her between us. We take her in her mouth, her pussy, and even her ass. We've always wanted a wife but knew that she would have to accept our way of life. There are couples here in Blessing who are living like we want to live."

She took a deep breath. How was she supposed to understand when she didn't even have a clue how a normal couple had sex, let alone two men sharing a woman?

"I'm sorry. You'll have to forgive me, but no one has even really explained to me how sex works. Babies are created between a man and a woman, but even my experience there is lacking."

The two men glanced at each other and she could see they were communicating without saying a word. They were indeed good friends.

Noel took her other hand. "The basic definition is that a man inserts his penis into a woman's pussy and they have sex. When he comes, his seed floods her vagina and sometimes a child is created. But there is so much more to the act. That's what would have happened to you in the whorehouse. But we want it to be special with our wife. We want to make certain she enjoys being with the two of us. We want her to love us and have our children."

There was so much more to this than what she understood.

"If we marry you, one of us will be your legal husband, but both of us would claim you. You would be ours and we would expect you to obey us or we would spank you," August said.

Spank her? She hadn't had a spanking since she was eight years old and Mrs. Griffin caught her stealing a cookie from the kitchen. That was back when cookies were made for them. Mr. Stephens had ended all the extras they received.

"I'm a grown woman. Why would you spank me?"

Noel stared at her, his sapphire eyes were almost mesmerizing. "We would spank you for pleasure and also to discipline you. You're our wife. We want you to obey us."

Christmas was not used to being disrespectful. The last couple of years, she had been the main caregiver for the children at the orphanage. Her chest filled with pain as she thought of the kids and wondered how they were doing. Had Jennifer stepped up and taken over her duties?

Would Mr. Stephens eventually sell Jennifer as well?

With a sigh, she glanced between the men.

"I always dreamed of marrying for love. Not necessity. You, August, don't even like me," she said.

"That's not true," August said. "It's just I had plans to fuck someone tonight and those plans were interrupted. Now I know Noel will not let me fuck you until you're married. But that doesn't mean I don't like you. In fact, honey, I'm very attracted to you."

Noel laughed. "She figured you out. I told you, you were being selfish."

"Maybe so, but this was my present to myself and I didn't get what I wanted," he said.

The man sounded selfish and petty, and what would life be like married to both men? Could she fall in love with them? Bear their children and be their wife?

There was shouting in the street below and they heard footsteps on the stairs.

Noel reached over and turned out the lantern, flooding the room in darkness.

Were they searching for her? They sat motionless until the footsteps walked on past the door. Breathing a sigh of relief, she realized, sitting in the darkness, she felt so nervous.

Nervous that Mrs. Leake's men would find her and uncertain about marrying, not one man, but two.

Sure, she had wanted Noel to marry her, but both men? How was that possible?

Did she have a choice? She wanted to sleep on it before she agreed to marry them. Two husbands who would teach her to live a life she'd never considered.

"I have two questions."

"Who will be the father of our children?"

"Both of us," they said with a grin.

"Where do you live?"

"We have a ranch not far from town. We have a nice home and barn, and today, we came in to buy cattle."

"Instead, we found a wife," August said.

Glancing away in the darkness, she sighed. This would never be a normal marriage, but then again, if she worked for the whorehouse, life would never be normal again.

"Can I please have tonight to think about what I want?" she asked, her voice barely a whisper. "The last two days have been a whirlwind. I'd just like to rest before I make my final decision."

"Of course," Noel said.

"Instead of cattle, we're coming home with a wife."

"Maybe," she said in the darkness. "Maybe."

CHAPTER 4

*T*he next morning, August rose from bed and glanced over at Christmas curled on her side. Her dark hair splayed across the pillow and her full lips slightly parted beckoned him.

From the moment he saw her, he'd been attracted, but he'd wanted to take her right there in the whorehouse and then leave her. But, oh no, Noel was a noble man who couldn't stand to see her being auctioned off like a piece of meat.

August had no problem in taking advantage of the woman. Young, beautiful with emerald eyes and long dark lashes that lay against her pale skin. No, he didn't want to harm her, but he didn't see a way out of her becoming a whore.

Unless one of them married her.

It wasn't that he didn't want to, but he just would like the opportunity to get to know her a little better before they committed their lives to her. Noel could be the more spontaneous of the two while August was the wilder. But even he balked at the idea of saying I do before they had a chance to court her.

His friend had a much better heart than August and was known for defending those unable to help themselves. Maybe that was why they were such good friends.

Maybe August had needed his help in crawling out of a bottle of pity. He wasn't the first man to ride west to escape his demons. And Noel had showed him life here could be good and that he didn't need his family, though he missed them something fierce.

Especially during the holidays. The holidays were about spending time with those you loved and now August had no one. Not after his father had disowned him.

As he glanced at the woman, he smiled at her name. Christmas. There must be some sort of significance for why they called her a religious name.

She moaned in her sleep and rolled over before her large emerald eyes opened and stared at him. "I thought that I dreamed last night."

"No," August said. "Would you like some coffee?"

"Yes," she said, raising in the bed, the dress dipping dangerously low to show a well-formed breast. One that he would have loved to suck into his mouth.

Damn, all he wanted on this trip was a chance to fuck a woman in the whorehouse and to buy some cattle. Now he wasn't certain he even wanted to buy cattle. At the moment, he just wanted to crawl in that bed and slip between her legs and pound his dick in that virginal pussy.

Noel raised from the settee where he had spent the night. "Did I hear someone mention coffee?"

"Yes, I thought I would go out and get some," August said, knowing that if he couldn't get in bed with Christmas, then he wanted a strong drink to wake him up.

"Good and check to see if anyone is around asking about Christmas. Somehow we need to slip her out of the hotel."

But where would she go? The woman said she had nowhere to stay. She was so gorgeous and August knew if she came home with them, he would soon be fucking her. And sneaking her out was going to be darn near impossible with the dress she was wearing.

Sitting up in bed, she stared at the two men.

"I've thought about it all night long," she said with a sigh. "If you will have me, I'm willing to become your wife. Both of you."

Was this what August really wanted? Yes, he knew Noel wanted to save her and help her the moment he saw her, but marrying her? At least if Noel married her, August could back out if this was not what he wanted.

Noel smiled. "Then today is our wedding day."

"If we can get her out of here," August said. "Let me go get coffee and I'll see what I can find out."

Grabbing his hat, he turned and glanced back at the sight of Christmas still lying in bed. Walking away from her was hard. When he closed the door behind him, he noticed a man standing down the hallway who glanced back at him.

"Morning," he said.

"Morning," the dark figure said. This couldn't be good. They were watching.

August continued on down the hall, going right past the man, getting a good look at his face. If there was trouble, he wanted to remember what the man looked like.

"Hey, you wouldn't have seen a dark-haired woman in a white dress, would you?"

Shit, it was one of the madam's henchmen searching for Christmas.

"Nope, I sure haven't," he said. "What did she do? Steal some cowboy blind?"

The man shook his head. "She's gone missing from the whorehouse."

"Oh," August said. "Those women are easily replaced."

"That's what I said, but the madam says she owes money," the man said with a shrug.

"Well, good luck finding her," he said as he continued walking down the hall, knowing if he returned to the room right now, the man would be suspicious.

As he walked out of the hotel into the bright sunshine, he noticed there were quite a few men lingering on the street corners. He continued on down the main avenue like he didn't notice them, but worried how would they get her out of the hotel.

When he reached the church, he talked to the pastor and told him they would be arriving later for a wedding. Next he went to a dressmaker and bought Christmas a new dress. Every woman deserved a new dress for her special day, but Christmas needed one because her dress would identify her immediately.

A genteel woman did not wear a dress like Christmas was wearing.

After he purchased all the undergarments, he went to the men's side and bought a pair of pants and shirt and a hat hopefully big enough to cover all that dark hair.

Then he stopped at the cafe and purchased three coffees. With his arms loaded down with garment bags and a pot of coffee and cups, he hurried back up to the room.

The man was gone when he walked down the hall.

"Open the door," he whispered, hoping that Christmas was nowhere near where the man might see her if he happened to spring out of nowhere.

Noel opened the door and unloaded his hands of the coffee pot and cups.

"Close it," he demanded and Noel looked at him and then glanced down the hall before he closed and locked the door.

"When I left this morning, there was a man who asked me about Christmas," he said. "As I walked to the church, there were men on every corner looking for her. The town is crawling with the madam's henchmen. They want her back. They say she owes the madam money."

"I do not," Christmas said, pouring herself a cup of the coffee.

Right now, August wasn't even certain on how they could get her to the church to marry her. There were more guns on the street than he'd ever seen.

"Wait a minute, didn't you say the director of the orphanage sold you to the madam?"

"Yes," Christmas said, her emerald eyes wide with fear.

"That's why she wants you. She paid money to the director for you. Plus, they don't want you out letting everyone know their scheme."

"Do you know if there are other girls who are missing?"

A tear slipped down her cheek. "Yes, but I thought they left in the middle of the night on their own accord. They were all old enough to leave."

The two men glanced at each other. She was not the first one and this must be quite the money-making plot for the director and also for the madam.

"What a winning deal for the orphanage," Noel said.

"Yes," Christmas said. "I didn't understand what was happening."

"How long has this been going on?" August asked.

"Mrs. Griffin died two years ago. It started about six months later. First Mary, then Georgia, Jean, and Brenda. Now I understand what happened."

The two men nodded. "Did you see any of the girls while you were there?"

"Only one, Mary," she almost whispered. "They kept me in a back room until a couple of hours before the sale. Then they bathed me and made me put on this horrible dress."

August grinned at her. "Darling, it looks really nice on you. It showed off your curves to perfection. Curves I can't wait to explore."

A blush spread across her cheeks and her head dipped before she stared at the two men. "It's indecent."

"Yes, it is," Noel said. "But we like to see you in it. It makes us want to touch your body."

The two men advanced on her and her eyes grew wide, her cheeks turned a sweet shade of pink.

Noel put his hands on her waist and then slid them up to her breasts. "Honey, these breasts are really nice."

He squeezed them with his hands. "As your husbands, we're going to enjoy them."

She gasped.

August ran his hands up the inside of the split in her dress, against her naked flesh. "Darling, your skin is soft as silk and I can't wait to have your legs wrapped around my waist as I shove my cock into your sweet pussy."

Her emerald eyes darkened with desire and August could

see she was not immune to passion. And yet he knew that last night she'd been terrified. But who wouldn't be? Taken from the orphanage against her will and then sold to the highest bidder.

Now August couldn't help but thank God that Noel had insisted they save her.

"You'll go slow with me?"

It was all August could do not to laugh. With her sweet body between them, it would be hard to go slow.

"We'll do our best," Noel said to her. "We need to get going. Somehow we've got to get to the church and then out of town without these goons seeing us."

August nodded. "It's not going to be easy. In fact, maybe the two of you should sneak to the church and I'll get the horses and rent a wagon for us to take home."

"Shouldn't we go to the sheriff?" Christmas asked. "I'd like to tell him about the orphans."

Oh goodness, the orphans were being left alone with the director who didn't have any business being around children.

The two men sighed. "She's right. We need to speak to the sheriff."

The thought of walking out of the hotel and down the street to the sheriff was gut wrenching. Could they make it without one of the henchmen recognizing her?

"I bought you a dress and also some men's clothes," August told her. "The men's clothes would be a good disguise."

Though how he thought her curves could be hidden he didn't know.

August pulled the dress out of the sack and she gasped. Tears sprang into her eyes. "I've never had a new dress before. May I please wear it?"

The thought of his sisters and the many new dresses they each received made his chest ache. This woman had no one and never had anything new. That was going to change. As his wife, she would have whatever she wanted. No, this marriage was not his idea and yet he liked Christmas. He liked her a lot. Maybe marrying her was a good idea after all, he thought as he handed her the garment.

"Thank you, I've always worn hand me downs, never a new dress," she said, holding the dress up to her. "It looks perfect."

The two men glanced at one another.

"Are you sure I can't wear it now?"

"No, darling, there are men out on the street looking for you. Wear the pants and when we get to the church, you can change," Noel said.

She ran to August and threw her arms around him, pressing her breasts into his chest. He almost choked up at the way she responded to his gift. No one had ever acted that way about something he bought them before.

She kissed his cheek. "Thank you. I will be the best wife I can be to you."

A lump formed in his throat and he hugged her back. No one had ever been more excited to receive something from him. All his life, he'd been raised never wanting for anything, getting into trouble, and causing shame to his family and yet Christmas accepted him.

Reaching down, he wiped the tears from her cheeks. "We've got to keep you safe. Go get dressed in the men's clothing and when we all get to the church, you can change."

Letting go of him, she reached into the sack and pulled out a brand-new shirt and pair of pants along with a hat.

"These are really nice too, but I do love the dress," she said.

A knock sounded on the door and they all froze.

"Yes," Noel said.

"It's the desk clerk," a young male's voice said. "Check out is eleven and it's ten till."

"Sorry," Noel said. "We overslept. We'll be down in about five minutes."

August shook his head. Fear gripped him as he realized this would be a great time to ambush them.

"You two go out the back door and I'll go downstairs and check us out," he said, putting everything back in sacks. "Let me take the dress. If anyone questions me, I can say it's for my sister."

Christmas stepped behind the screen and when she came out, they both whistled. "Now that's a damn fine-looking man."

Noel laughed and helped her put her hair up inside the hat. "We're going first to the sheriff's office and then we'll go to the church."

August was afraid for them all. He didn't like being separated from his friend and Christmas, but if there were three of them, then others would question whether or not it was her.

Christmas walked over to August. "Be careful and we'll see you at the church."

She leaned in and kissed him on the cheek.

Damn, if she kept doing that, he was going to have a hard time keeping his heart from getting involved.

"You too," he said. "You both go first and then I'll go down to the desk."

Opening the door, he signaled them when the hall was clear. They hurried down the hall and out the back door.

After he had gathered their belongs, he made his way down to the desk. Two rough looking cowboys were standing near the door as he walked up to the counter.

"Where's your friend?" the clerk asked.

"Oh, he had to leave early this morning to meet with the cattle broker. I'm headed back to our ranch."

The kid's forehead wrinkled in a frown.

"Lot of packages you got there," he said.

The man was fishing for information and trying to tie him to the missing girl.

"I have a younger sister at home. Her birthday is coming up and I wanted to get her a new dress."

The man sighed and checked him out, took his money and then glanced at the gentlemen near the door.

"Thank you, Mr. Hamilton."

"Thanks and you men have a great day," he said as he walked out.

That was close. Damn close and he wasn't certain they hadn't followed him. Somewhere between the livery stable and the church, he'd need to lose them.

CHAPTER 5

*W*hen they walked into the alley, she could see suspicious men near the street.

"Walk a little stiffer," Noel told her. "Don't let your hips roll like a woman."

"Easier said than done," she told him as she tried not to sway from side to side like she'd seen the boys in the orphanage do when they were becoming men. But her hips wanted to roll.

As they walked past the men, Noel smiled at them. "Morning, gentlemen."

"Morning," they said.

They glanced at Christmas, but she ducked her head into her chest as they continued onto the busy Main Street of Helena.

"Good," Noel said. "Let's go to the sheriff's office."

As they turned onto the street where his office was, Christmas saw a sign on the door. "Oh no, he's gone."

"Don't stop," Noel said. "Walk on past the door like we're

going somewhere else. We've got a man following us. We're going into the mercantile."

When they walked past the sheriff's office, they saw a note that said he wouldn't return until Wednesday. So where was his deputy?

Two doors down, they walked into the store. The man stepped in behind them.

"What was it your mother asked us to get?" Noel asked.

"Flour so she could make some cookies before Christmas," she said back to him, trying to make her voice sound rough and deep.

Noel smiled at her. "Is that all she needed?"

"Yes," she replied.

Noel laid the bag of flour on the counter and then he paid the man who stood gazing at the two of them, his eyes narrowed. It was Mr. Bailey and he was one of the biggest gossips in town.

"You from around here?"

"Nope," Noel said. "We come into town occasionally, but we don't live here."

The man nodded. "Come back in whenever you visit."

Noel turned and walked straight to the man following them. He stopped and stared at him while Christmas kept her head down. She was not about to look the man in the face.

Fear gripped her and she was afraid he would knock her hat to the ground and her hair would come spilling out.

"Morning," Noel said, clearly letting the man know he knew he was following him. "Are you lost?"

The man shook his head. "No, just needed to stop in and get some supplies."

"Good day," Noel said and they walked around the man and hurried out the door.

When they got outside, Noel pulled them into an alley and they waited. Soon the man came out of the store and glanced around, looking for them.

"Sucker," Noel said beneath his breath.

When the man finally walked on, they picked up their pace and headed along back streets to the church.

The closer they came to the church, the more frightened Christmas became. What was she doing? She knew nothing about Noel and August and yet she was about to marry Noel.

Marriage was forever and she feared that she was making a big mistake. But what choice did she have? And he seemed like such a nice man.

When they entered the church, August was waiting for them just inside the door.

She'd visited this church many times and she gazed at the sanctuary.

"I was beginning to get worried," he said.

"Me too," Noel told him. "We had to get rid of a man following us."

"Yes, me too," August said. "The wagon is sitting behind the church. The horses are hitched and just as soon as you two say your vows, we're ready to go."

The pastor walked into the sanctuary. "Christmas," he said. "Where are the children?" She hugged the man and he gazed at her. "What's going on?"

For the next several minutes, she told him a little about what had happened to her, but she did not mention that Mr. Stephens was the one who sold her into the brothel. She couldn't risk the children's safety. She couldn't take a chance that the pastor would tell Mr. Stephens the preposterous things Christmas was saying about him.

The old man's eyes narrowed. "You're not the first girl to wake up there. Have you spoken to the sheriff?"

Christmas shook her head. "He's not in his office and the deputy was not there either."

The man nodded and then he gazed at the two men who sat waiting patiently for her. "Who are you marrying? Are you certain about this, Christmas?"

No, she wasn't but her choices were limited. And Noel and August seemed like nice men. She could do a lot worse. Still, the thought of being married to not one, but two men was enough to make her tremble inside.

Gazing at Noel, she sighed. The man was extremely handsome with his dark hair and thick arms, along with muscled chest and thighs. In some ways, he reminded her of a Viking lord she had read about in books.

"I'm marrying Noel Brooks. Yes, I am certain," she said, surprising herself. "Could I change into the dress that August bought for me. And then will you marry us?"

She couldn't believe the words managed to come from her, but she felt certain she was doing what was right. For everyone. It was like a sense of peace came over her and she knew this was meant to be.

The pastor's face smiled. "Of course. You go change and I'll talk to Mr. Brooks."

The reverend had always been good to the orphans and he pushed his members to help out the orphanage by giving to them. Now she wondered where the donation money was going. Could the reason things had gotten so much tighter taking care of the children be because Stephens was pocketing the donations as well?

Their lives would be a lot worse if not for the preacher and she hated that she couldn't tell him all of the truth. But right now, she needed to keep things to herself and her husbands, including that Mr. Stephens was the one selling the young girls to the whorehouse.

She felt blessed to have been rescued by Noel and August but feared for Jennifer's life, certain she would be next. And what about the others that had gone missing? Where were they?

In a back room, she pulled the new dress out of the bag, tears welling in her eyes. It was green with off-the-shoulder sleeves and little bows. The man had also purchased a petticoat and chemise, but she could not find bloomers.

Why did it seem like no one wore bloomers anymore?

Quickly she dressed and stood before the mirror gazing at herself. She looked like a fine lady. Like one of the women who came to the orphanage and brought them toiletry items and gifts.

Someday she hoped that she could help the orphanage. Someday...

Tears fell as she stared at herself. Today she would be a bride and soon a wife. She said a quick prayer asking that her marriage to both men be a good one.

She still didn't understand how this would work, but at least she would not be giving her body to random men in a brothel.

With a deep breath, she put the men's clothes back in the bag before she stepped out of the room.

As she walked to the men and the pastor, they all stopped and stared.

"You're beautiful," Noel said. "I'm a lucky man that you are going to be my wife."

The man was so sweet. Smiling up at him, she whispered. "Thank you."

August just gazed at her with his mouth open. "Beautiful. Noel is a getting a sweet wife."

Though she was only marrying one of the men, she knew they would both consider her married to them. And in many ways, she felt lucky.

The pastor smiled at her. "Are you ready?"

"Yes," she said. "And pastor you can't tell anyone that I was here today and that I married. They're searching for me."

The elderly man patted her on the arm.

"I know," he said. "Your husband was just telling me."

Ten minutes later, after they said their vows, the pastor smiled at her and Noel. "You may kiss your bride."

Stunned, she turned toward him as his lips came down on hers, his hands gripping her cheeks as his lips moved over hers, claiming her as his wife.

A heat began to build inside her like something she'd never experienced. What was happening?

His lips were soft and smooth and she liked kissing her husband.

Suddenly, he broke the kiss. "Congratulations, Mrs. Brooks."

Warmth flooded her face as she stared at her new husband. "May our life together be blessed."

The pastor smiled. "Congratulations. I'm happy for you, Christmas."

With a nod, she gazed at Noel and grinned.

"I'm not trying to rush you, but the sun is starting to sink in the sky and it would be best if you were out of town before dark."

"Yes," August said. "The wagon is in back. Sorry, Christmas, but you need to change clothes and lie down in the bed of the wagon. I'm going to cover you until we get out of town."

With a sigh, she went into the dressing room and put on the men's clothes.

When she walked out, the pastor shook his head. "Be careful. I'll contact the sheriff and ask him to go see you."

"Would you please check on the children? I'm worried about them," she said, knowing Jennifer would care for them, but she still worried.

He smiled. "Of course. Now go."

Just then there came a pounding at the front door. "Pastor, we need to speak to you."

"Go out the back, now," he told them, rushing them to the back of the church.

Terror gripped her chest as they ran out the rear, carefully checking to make certain no one was watching.

With a sigh, she realized she was heading to her new life as a wife. Tonight would be her wedding night and she would no longer be a virgin. No longer would the madam have a reason to sell her.

CHAPTER 6

*N*oel didn't wait to see who was pounding on the door of the church. After she changed, he took Christmas by the arm, and together, the three of them slunk out the back door. They had to hurry.

In the last rays of the sun, the men put her in the back of the wagon, covered her and then climbed up on the seat.

Noel clicked to the horses and tried to drive like it was a normal evening for them to be leaving town. But it was anything but normal. It was their wedding night. And he would do anything necessary to protect his new wife. Anything.

She now belonged to him and August and they would die protecting her. The madam didn't know who she was coming after if she learned of their marriage.

When they hit the main road, he noticed groups of men on horses watching everyone who left town.

"Hey," a man called to them.

"What?" Noel called, the sun glaring in his eyes.

"What do you have in your wagon?"

"Supplies, groceries and a couple of spools of rope. Why?"

The man started toward the wagon and Noel knew he would throw the tarp back and that wasn't going to happen.

He flipped the reins and acted like he didn't realize the man was coming at him.

"Stop," the man yelled, but Noel ignored him, though he did push the horses a little faster toward home.

Once they had gone a mile, he glanced behind them and saw no one. It appeared they weren't pursuing them, which was strange. Maybe acting like he didn't know what they wanted had worked. But he wasn't going to stop.

"They really want her," August said.

"Too bad," Noel replied, thinking it would be a cold day in hell before they took Christmas from them. "She's our wife now."

The two men glanced at each other and smiled. Tonight was their wedding night and Noel could hardly wait. Christmas was an innocent and he couldn't wait to show her the joys of sex.

When the sun had sunk below the horizon, they continued on, but August did lean back and pull the tarp off Christmas to give her more air.

"Is it safe?" Christmas asked. "I was so frightened they were going to stop us."

"You and me both," Noel said.

"Just lie there until we get home," August told her. "Let's not take a chance on someone seeing you sitting up here on the bench beside us."

Noel completely agreed. There was no point in them risking Christmas getting hurt or anyone else.

"All right," she said. "Tell me about your home."

Noel smiled at the thought of the spread that he and August shared, pleased she would ask. "We have over one hundred acres with cattle, horses, and chickens. You'll be in charge of the chickens."

"Fresh eggs," she said with a sigh.

"Yes," August replied. "We have a three-bedroom house and a bunkhouse that can sleep ten, for whenever we hire hands, we'll have room for them."

"We built the house ourselves, but we tried to think of things that a woman would like. You're the first woman to step foot inside our home."

"It sounds heavenly compared to the orphanage. A real home."

Noel had not considered what it felt like to have no place to call your own. No, his family had not been wealthy, but they had been happy and he missed them. Oh, how he missed them. But when he thought of returning, he would see Sadie's face and know he couldn't go home.

When seeing their land, Noel felt his chest tighten. The house always made his insides warm at the realization he was home.

It was a cute place where a family could live. A family filled with love for each other. That's what he wanted more than anything.

He pulled the wagon up in front of the house. "I drove, so you put the horses away and I'll carry Christmas over the threshold."

August sighed but jumped out of the wagon and went to help Christmas alight. He pulled her to sitting and then he helped her out of the wagon. "Go with Noel. I'll be there soon. Don't start without me."

Noel took Christmas by the arm and they strolled to the door of the house before he swept her up in his arms.

"Oh, what are you doing?"

"I'm carrying you over the threshold, Mrs. Brooks. That's what married couples do the first time they enter their home."

She wrapped her arms around his neck and gazed at him. Heat spread like a wildfire through him at the feel of her body snug against his own. The way her breasts rubbed against his chest, the smell of her, all sweet woman snuggled in his arms.

Tonight was all about giving her pleasure and he wanted to make certain that she enjoyed the experience of both of her husbands. He liked her full breasts and tiny waist and legs that could wrap around a man's body and ride him like a horse.

He loved the way her emerald eyes would flash with annoyance or be subtle in the way they shifted and filled with passion.

Yet, as much as he wanted her, he had to remember that this has been awfully quick. Maybe she needed a little more time. But he hoped not. Tonight he wanted to claim her every way possible. Make her theirs.

"Are you all right with us being together tonight or do you want to wait?"

Shaking her head, she sighed. "No, we're married. If the marriage is consummated, no one can take me from you. You and August are my husbands. Let's start our marriage off right."

As much as he'd like to believe once they took her virginity, she'd be safe, he knew that if the madam's henchmen found her, they would do everything they could to take her. No, they needed to speak to the sheriff and tell him what was happening at the orphanage. They needed to make certain the madam knew that Christmas belonged to them and they would not tolerate her interference. They needed Christmas.

He set her on the floor and kissed her. Her lips were soft and pliable and she leaned into him, pressing up against his hard cock and that surprised him.

Suddenly her eyes widened and she broke the kiss with a gasp.

"I'm sorry."

"For what?"

"For…"

A pretty blush spread across her face and she ducked her head.

He lifted her chin so her eyes met his. "Never be embarrassed. I'm hard because I'm attracted to you. As my wife, that's a great thing. What we're going to do tonight will be new for you, but we're married and it's all right. If something makes you uncomfortable, tell us and we'll talk about it. But we want you, as our wife, to want us just as much as we desire you."

From her expression, he could tell she had no idea about desiring a man, but tonight she would learn.

She licked her lips nervously. "Thank you for marrying me."

"My pleasure," he said, thinking how he couldn't wait much longer to take her.

If only she knew what she did to both of them, she wouldn't have to say thank you. They wanted her and he was just thrilled they found her, though it was rather hazardous to their health. And even now, he feared a visit from the madam's henchmen.

But they knew how to defend their place. How to defend their woman.

"Why don't you go upstairs, remove all your clothing and we'll be up very soon," he said, discerning that if August didn't return soon, he was going in search for him.

"All right," she said, hurrying up the stairs.

Where was that man? Didn't he realize it was their wedding night? Just then the door opened and he strolled in.

"Wind's kicking up. Looks like we got home before a northerner hit. It's going to be cold, but we'll be all snuggled up here inside with Christmas." He glanced around. "Where is she?"

Noel smiled. "I sent her upstairs to prepare for us. All we're waiting on is you."

"Are you certain about this?" August asked him. "It's not too late to back out."

It was hard to believe he was still having doubts, but once they claimed Christmas, he knew August would come around.

Noel had no doubts about what he'd done today. Not only had they saved Christmas from the whorehouse, but he felt like he'd found a woman who would eventually be everything he'd ever wanted.

Now they were married men. Married to a beauty of a woman who seemed to have a caring heart.

"I'm absolutely certain. Let's go. Our bride awaits," he said as he hurried up the stairs eager to see Christmas.

"I'm going to get some Christmas pussy," August said, following behind him. "Finally."

CHAPTER 7

*C*hristmas lay on the bed, anxiously waiting. She'd never been so nervous in all her life. The room she was in was very masculine and she wondered if it was here she would sleep or if they would put her in another room after they had sex.

Though they were married, she still was anxious. Tonight would be her first time and she had no idea what to expect.

Both men were handsome and she felt attracted to both, but what would it be like with two men? She knew so little and she didn't want to disappoint them. No matter what, she wanted to be a good wife. One they enjoyed taking pleasure with.

Noel walked in and glanced at her lying on the bed with the covers up around her neck.

"Oh, darling, tonight you're not going to need covers. We're going to make you so hot, you're going to think you're on fire."

What was he talking about? Hot? How?

Noel peeled his shirt out of his pants and then tossed it

onto a chair. He sank down into the chair and pulled off his boots and socks, then he removed his pants and long johns. The man was standing stark naked in front of her, caressing the hard penis that jutted out from his body.

Nervously she swallowed. Soon he would enter her body. Was she supposed to just lay there or what? What did they expect from her?

She glanced over to see August was the neater of the two. He folded his clothes before he turned to face her, his penis jutting out hard and rigid.

Oh my.

Shock and heat rippled through her and her center ached for something she didn't understand.

Their male bodies were strong, their muscles clearly defined as she gazed at their manhoods. Both were unique. Both made her heart beat faster. Both made her body crave something she didn't understand.

"Beautiful," Noel said as he stroked his cock, gazing at her. "You wife, are so innocent, your breasts are full and ripe and we can't wait to experience your pussy."

His words made her feel warm, like someone had lit a fire in her body.

For a moment, she stared. She'd never seen a man's personal parts and the long member fascinated her. Smooth, rigid, and hard and she longed to touch the very end. See how it felt when he slid the skin up and back.

"Tonight we're going to claim you. Make you ours," Noel said, walking close to her, his hand on his cock, stroking it, making it grow longer and harder.

"You're married to Noel, but you belong to both of us,"

August said, gazing at her as he stepped close and ripped the sheet from her fingers, exposing her breasts, her naked flesh.

Heat rippled through her as they stared at her body.

Automatically, her hands reached up to cover herself from his gaze, a whimper escaped from her throat. He removed her hands and then stepped back to stare at her breasts.

"Aww, Christmas," he said with a moan.

Warmth spread in her lower stomach. Anxieties overcame her and she reached up to cover her breasts again.

"No, honey, we're your men and we can't wait to explore every inch of you," Noel said in a soothing voice. "We're going to know your body better than you do."

His words caused her pulse to race, the center of her ached and her breathing became labored. What were they talking about? What would they do?

"Your skin feels like silk and we can't wait to know your body like we know our own," August said as his fingers skimmed over her breasts and he took her nipples between his fingers and twisted them.

A fiery heat spiraled through her and she gasped. The sensation of his fingers was creating feelings she'd never experienced.

"We want to hear you moan and scream our names as passion overtakes you," Noel said, moving onto the bed beside her.

He tossed the sheet to the floor and then stared down at her. Blood heated and pounded as it rushed through her, causing her lungs to squeeze as she gasped for breath at the thought of them touching her.

"Oh, August, she has a sweet looking pussy."

His hand slid down her chest, past her waist until he reached between her legs, his fingers sliding over her folds.

Pleasure like a warm river rippled through her and she gasped. "Noel."

"Honey, you're dripping wet," he said. "We've just started. I think you like what we're doing to you."

What could she say? August leaned in closer as his mouth came down on hers. This was not a sweet kiss, but one that demanded she surrender. Demanded she give herself to him as he ravaged her mouth, making her shiver as a feeling built inside her. His tongue pushed its way inside her mouth, and he explored her while Noel's fingers continued to stroke her clit. Never had she felt so many emotions at once.

So much heat.

Noel continued to stroke her pussy lips, slipping a finger inside causing her breathing to almost cease as pleasure filled her. Pressure began to build inside her as she arched her back and moaned.

There were so many sensations. So many satisfactions that she didn't know what would happen next. August's lips broke from hers and he kissed her neck, her shoulders.

August whispered against her ear, his fingers sliding down her backside, down her crack, touching her in the most private area. "You have two men. We'll prepare you, but eventually, we'll both take you at the same time. One in your pussy and one in your ass."

"Oh," she cried as his fingers circled her anus sending a zing of passion through her, which surprised her. The heat that simple touch created left her gasping.

Why did his touch feel so good?

The men rolled her onto her side. One man was at her

back and the other her front and the friction she felt as their fingers stroked her was almost more than she could bear.

"What is this feeling?"

"You're about to come," August said. "Just go with the feelings. We're right here holding you, protecting and keeping you safe."

Whatever were they talking about? Come? She didn't understand and yet the pressure building inside her from the sensations they were creating was such a pleasant experience. She moaned as she lay between them.

"I'm going to spank your pussy," Noel whispered in her ear.

What was he talking about?

Suddenly she felt a stinging between her legs and yet it wasn't a bad feeling, but rather one that had her body tensing and she moaned.

"Come, baby, come for us," Noel said as he slapped her pussy again.

This time, an explosion of color filled her as her body tensed and she moaned as she spasmed beneath their fingers.

Like a tightly strung string, she gasped as her body rippled beneath their hands.

For a moment, they gave her a respite as she lay there trying to catch her breath and slowly coming back to her senses.

"You just had your first orgasm," August said, grinning above her. "This one will be even better."

Rolling her onto her back, he lifted her legs into the air and spread them. His fingers pulled apart her pussy lips and his mouth descended on her, his tongue lapping at her folds.

"August," she cried as a convulsion of explosion zipped through her. "Oh, August."

What was he doing to her? She had never considered a man putting his mouth on her womanly parts.

"Your cunt tastes sweeter than honey," he said as he began to lick her faster, his tongue pushing up inside her, creating a spasm that had her moaning and shaking.

Once again, the pleasure built inside her, ready to explode and she didn't know how to handle the feeling. Was this what married people did?

Noel pressed his finger into her back entrance, insistent and sure. The feel of that finger probing her, swirling and demanding entry, sent her spiraling out of control. She screamed as the world around her shattered. Her men held her as her body tensed and she bucked and felt like she would faint.

This time when it ended, she glanced in awe at them. "Is it always this intense?"

"Only when it's good," Noel said as he moved to hold her.

"Honey, we're so pleased that you like my finger in your ass. Soon it will be my cock."

It was true. Never would she have imagined that the feelings of hunger, the insistent need for him to stroke her, would overpower her objections. Never would she object if this was what her husbands wanted. Because she liked the feel of his finger but worried what his cock would feel like.

August smiled. "She came all over my face," he said with a grin. "Nothing sweeter."

"We've waited long enough. It's time to make you ours," Noel said.

"Since I married her, you get the honors of taking her

maidenhead," Noel said as he glanced at August. "But I call dibs on taking her ass first. Not tonight, but soon. I can't wait for us both to claim you together."

As much as Christmas was trying to understand what they were saying, she didn't really know what Noel meant. Right now, she just trusted them to keep her safe and make her feel so good.

August lay down on the bed beside Christmas. "The first time always hurts, but it won't last long."

Noel pulled her on top of him. Her back to his chest and August crawled on the bed over her. She was sandwiched between the two men and moaned at the feel of their naked flesh against her own. Noel's firm chest supported her body and August leaned over her.

The heat generated between them had her breathing hard and eager for them to take her.

August's long, hard dick jutted out like a sword. Never had she considered two men before and now she couldn't imagine sex any other way. The feel of being sandwiched between them was nothing like she'd ever experienced. It was like they enfolded her into their bodies.

Like they protected her and shielded her from whatever life would give them. She was their woman and tonight they were making her theirs.

August placed his long, rigid penis at the entrance to her pussy and suddenly fear spiraled through her.

A whimper escaped her before Noel reached down, parted the folds between her legs, and rubbed the little nub. Pleasure spiked through her and she moaned and lifted her hips as if to urge him to fuck her. Take her now before she changed her mind.

Though she tried to relax, she was nervous as August moved forward. Slowly he entered her pussy while his fingers continued to rub her and she groaned. Suddenly she felt him reach the wall of resistance.

After this moment, she would never be a virgin again. After tonight, she would belong to Noel and August.

With a quick thrust, she experienced a jolt of pain. For a moment, she tensed and then she began to relax.

It was over.

Lying on top of her, he didn't move as the stinging subsided. She groaned as she felt her body stretching to accept his long cock as he filled her.

"You're so big," she whimpered.

"Yes, darling, I am," August said. "This time, I want you to scream my name when you come. Don't come until I say you can."

Fear filled her as he began to move, but this time, heat exploded inside her. The friction of him pushing in was creating a whole new set of sensations she had no idea existed.

Reaching down, she grabbed his hips and tried to make him move faster. This time, she needed him. She wanted him to pound his cock inside her and give her the relief she sought.

"Darling, we go at my pace," he said with a gasp.

"Faster," she cried.

A chuckle came from August. "No."

With a whimper, she tried to calm the urges inside her. Soon he was completely within her, but he pulled out and she raised her hips, needing, wanting more. Wanting to scream *put it back*.

Noel's fingers plunged inside her back entrance, sending a jolt of pleasure through her. With a cry, she rose and met August and dropped down on Noel's fingers.

"Open up for me. Take me inside your ass. Let us give you pleasure."

Heat and fire built inside her until she feared she would explode and disintegrate right there in their arms. Noel pushed a second finger inside her rectum and she squealed at the pain-pleasure that erupted inside her. They rocked her back and forth between them and the heat inside her continued to build. The fire raged and then she felt her orgasm like a tsunami roaring toward her.

"I can't hold back. I'm going to come," she gasped.

"Scream my name and you may come," August said as he pounded into her pussy.

"August," she screamed as she clenched his cock inside her tightly, squeezing it. Waves of pleasure filled her, and for a moment, she felt like she would drown as she gulped for air. August gave one last push as his seed exploded inside her, coating her pussy walls.

Christmas slumped in Noel's arms. Tonight she could become pregnant. She could have a baby. The thought gripped her.

When glancing into Noel's eyes, he smiled at her. "My turn."

"Oh," she said, wondering how she could do this again.

She rolled onto her back as Noel stood. "No, I want to take you from behind. I want to see your ass twitch as I shove my cock in your pussy. I want to spank your ass as you come."

He was going to spank her? Why?

Rolling over, she moved up on her hands and knees before she glanced back at him.

"Darling, you screamed August's name, now I want to hear mine."

He slapped her ass not hard, but with enough force that she felt it jar all the way to her pussy. "Noel."

"One more time," he said as his hand connected with her ass. It burned but the heat created a fire inside her. A fire that centered in her middle. A fire that she realized would soon be an inferno.

Spanking her was shocking. She didn't expect his hand smacking her ass would arouse her, but it did. It was like all the other things they'd done to her multiplied by ten and she moaned.

Noel pushed her head down and August helped her into the position they wanted her. Her head rested on her arms, with her ass sticking up in the air.

"Darling, you have the cutest little ass. All pink from my hand, your pussy dripping with want and your ass just begging for my finger."

His words had her moaning. It was all true. She wanted his finger in her ass. She wanted Noel.

"Beg me for it."

"Please fuck me," she said, thinking that was the only thing he wanted. And it worked.

August's mouth covered hers as Noel placed his hands around her hips and moved her in pace with his fucking. Noel hammered into her, time after time, his cock once again causing her to heat with desire. Would it always be this way between them?

The bed squeaked, the mattress hitting the back wall as Noel pounded into her.

"Don't come," he commanded.

She bit her lip, trying to stop the need to explode all over his cock. "I can't…"

Smack! He hit her ass with his palm. He lifted her hips to meet him and she could feel a scream building inside.

Never would she have dreamed that having sex was anything like what they were doing, but now she couldn't imagine it any other way.

"Come now," he cried as his seed exploded inside her, coating her pussy walls.

And she did. A scream tore from her throat as she cried out, "Noel."

He held her against him while she writhed and convulsed in his arms. Finally, they collapsed onto the bed. Totally spent, she lay there, knowing she would never be the same. Her men arranged her body until she lay between them.

Her chest to Noel's back and August's chest to her back. The feel of their hard bodies next to hers had heat sliding through her once again.

Maybe marrying them had been the best decision she'd ever made. Maybe being their wife would give her the life she so desperately wanted. Maybe she could help the others she had left behind.

"This is how it will always be. You between the two of us."

"We will always take care of you," Noel said.

Tonight she would thank God for rescuing her from the bordello. Tonight she would ponder how she could save the other orphans.

Reaching out, she took each man's hand and brought it up

to her lips to kiss. "Thank you. Thank you for marrying me. When can we do that again?"

Both men laughed. "I think she likes having sex."

"Oh, yes," she said with a sigh. "Definitely want to do that again."

CHAPTER 8

 he next morning August awoke and the smell of sex and woman overwhelmed him. Last night came rushing back and he smiled. Christmas had been better than any woman he'd ever fucked. And this morning, he planned on starting his day off with her in his arms and his cock between her legs.

The bed moved as Noel rolled over, nude. He slipped his fingers between her legs and pulled them apart. She moaned in her sleep.

"I think she's dreaming of us," he said. "She's wet."

"Let's wake her up," August said, not wanting to wait a moment longer. Last night had convinced him that marrying Christmas had been the best decision Noel had ever made. All it took was one night and he'd become besotted with Christmas.

He trailed his lips across her lips, down her neck to her shoulder, where he lightly bit her.

She moaned and opened one large emerald eye and gazed at him. Then the second eye stared at him.

"Good morning, sunshine. It's time for you to learn to suck my cock."

Last night, he had not taught her what he enjoyed the most. This morning, she would soon learn the finer techniques of sucking a man's cock. And he couldn't wait to get started.

"What?"

He rolled her over, so her head hovered over his cock as he sat up against the headboard of the bed.

"Put your lips around my cock and suck on the head," August commanded. "Just like I licked your pussy last night."

And he'd enjoyed every moment of tasting her sweet little cunt. And even more shoving his cock deep in her and coming.

He pulled her head down to his cock and she opened her mouth. With a sigh, he felt her sweet lips touching the bulbous head of his cock.

"Now run your tongue around it and suck on the bulb," he said with a moan.

As she sucked on August's cock, Noel moved behind her. His fingers teased her clit.

She moaned and August jerked at the vibration that came when she moaned.

"Oh, darling, that feels so good. Twist her clitty again," he instructed Noel. "I like the way her mouth vibrated when she moaned."

Noel thrust his fingers up into her pussy and she groaned all over August's cock. His hands spread her cheeks as he placed his mouth against her pussy and she screamed.

"Oh, that feels good," August said, knowing if they kept this up, he wouldn't last much longer. The sensations of her reactions to what Noel was doing were rushing his climax toward fruition.

"Oh, darling, I'm getting ready to come," August said as he lay back and angled her mouth to receive him.

Noel's hands gripped her hips as his tongue worked its magic on her clit. She began to thrash her body, needing, wanting what they could give her.

August grabbed her hair and pushed his cock farther in her mouth as he moved her head up and down. Enjoying the feel of her lips as they sucked him.

"I'm going to come in your mouth, Christmas. Swallow it all," he said as he groaned, his body going rigid as he shoved his cock deeper into her throat. His orgasm was rushing at him like a herd of stampeding cattle and with one last shove, he was coming.

"Christmas," August cried, his seed filling her mouth.

The woman was learning and she swallowed every drop before she leaned her head on his chest.

"Noel, please," she cried, glancing at him over her shoulder as he pulled his mouth away and moved behind her. She leaned back, eager to receive his cock.

"What do you want, darling?"

"You, please, I need you," she cried.

August watched as Noel slammed into her pussy with his rock-hard cock and she groaned. For a moment, they moved in unison as he held her hips, rocking her exactly like he wanted.

Reaching for her breasts, August twisted her nipples and she gasped. While he played with her breasts, he watched his friend push his fingers into her back passage.

"Noel," she cried.

"What, darling? Do you like my finger in your ass?"

She glanced behind her at him and August knew she didn't want to admit it.

"Be honest with us," he whispered against her head. "Or you'll be punished."

"Yes, it feels so good," she moaned. "Oh," she cried as he began to stretch her even farther with a second finger.

"Christmas, let me in. Soon we're going to take you back here," Noel promised.

"Aargh," she cried. "Please, I need you."

August covered her mouth with his as Noel plunged three fingers in her and she moaned in his mouth.

She released August's mouth. "I'm going to come."

"Not yet. I'm not ready for us to come," Noel said, and he slapped her ass.

"Noel," she cried as she bit her lip.

"Just a little longer, darling. Grip my cock with your pussy," he said. "Oh yes, just like that."

August watched as his friend pounded into her pussy, his cock plunging in and out.

"Now, you may come," he said.

August knew Noel's seed was spilling into her womb and he prayed that she would soon be with child. He didn't care who the father was. As long as they had a large family to replace the one he'd been ejected from.

As long as Christmas bore their children.

She screamed with pleasure, her body shaking and undulating as the orgasm rocked her over and over while August held her.

Damn, but he loved fucking like this. Damn, this woman was more than even he ever thought she could be. Why he didn't want her at first, he didn't know, but now he would protect her with his life.

Christmas belonged to them and no one would ever take her from them and live to tell the tale.

Noel and Christmas collapsed onto the bed. The two men moved her until she was between them again. This time, they were on either side of her while they all lay in silence as they seemed to catch their breath.

"What a way to begin the day," August said, smiling from ear to ear. Maybe he didn't want to marry Christmas, but now he was so damn glad they had.

Noel grinned, stood, and walked to a dresser nearby. He opened the drawer and pulled out a razor and cup.

"Darling, we want your pussy to be gleaming. So, we're going to shave you and then we'll give you your first butt plug."

"What is a butt plug?"

"Something you wear in your ass to spread your muscles to accept us. This way you aren't hurt or in pain when we take you."

Rising, she gazed at the two men. "Do all married couples have this kind of sex life?"

Noel laughed. "Probably not, honey. But as long as we're all happy, who cares?"

They positioned her on the bed to where Noel could scrape the hair from her pussy.

"Spread your legs, darling," August said.

With the first brush of shaving cream, she moaned. "That tickles," she said.

The men looked at each other and smiled.

"Noel," she said, her voice nervous.

"Relax," he told her. "You're going to enjoy being shaved."

August noticed the way she was gripping the sheet in her hands. "Does it feel good, darling?"

"Yes," she cried just as the razor zipped the last bit of hair from her pussy.

She glanced down at her folds. "You can see everything."

"Yes," August told her. "I can't wait to kiss you down there."

She moaned.

"Now for the butt plug," Noel said, rising from the bed.

"Up on your knees," August demanded.

In a matter of moments, they put her into the position they wanted her. Complete obedience with her ass up in the air. After all, she belonged to them. They would do whatever was necessary to make them all happy.

August watched as his friend pushed lubricant into her ass and then spread her hips, exposing her back passage.

"Relax, Christmas," Noel said. "Soon, you won't need a butt plug. Soon, you'll be taking us both at the same time. I can't wait to shove my cock in your ass."

The sight of her ass spread as Noel prepared her made August's cock spring back to life.

"Hurry, I want to fuck her," August said, the desire overwhelming him at the sight of her pearly white ass quivering with anticipation as his partner pushed in the wooden dowel.

"Oh," she cried. "Please."

"All in," Noel said and gave her a smack on the ass.

"Aargh," she cried. "That vibrated."

Noel grinned. "I'm sure it did and I can't wait to do that again. Sometime today, I'm going to pull your skirts up and smack your ass just to give you pleasure."

"Oh," she cried.

"On your back and spread your legs," August commanded. His need urgent.

Gazing up at him, her emerald eyes were dark with passion as she stared at him.

"I'm not going to last long."

When she was in position, he pushed his cock into her sweet, shaved pussy. The lips were swollen and wet and with a groan, he stroked her.

"No, it's too much," she groaned. "Take the plug out. It's so tight."

There was no way he was going to take out the fullness that made her even tighter as she gripped his cock.

"Darling, relax. I promise, you're going to enjoy me fucking you with the butt plug in. It will be all right," Noel told her.

She took a deep breath and August noticed that her emerald eyes grew large with passion and her upper lip curled like she was fighting to keep from coming.

"All better," he asked, knowing he wouldn't last much longer. Her pussy was just so tight and gave his cock so much pleasure.

Noel reached down and sucked her breast into his mouth. She gripped the sheets. "Noel."

"Darling, is there something you need?"

"Oh yes, please, August, hurry," she gasped. "I don't think I can hold off—"

Noel leaned back, but kept his fingers on her nipples, twisting them.

August raised her legs over her shoulder as he pounded into her pussy and then he smacked the butt plug.

A shudder rippled through them both. "Christmas."

"August," she screamed as she came all over his cock.

Being married definitely had its advantages. August was so glad that Christmas had married them.

With one last shove, he flooded her pussy with his seed. With another shove, felt his body relax.

As he lowered her legs, he slumped over her body.

"Good morning," he said with a grin.

They lay there for a couple moments resting before the sun came up. Today was the beginning of their life together and he was so excited. Christmas was theirs and never would he give her up.

With a sigh, he rolled over and pulled her into his arms.

Suddenly a torch flew through the upstairs window, breaking the glass.

Stunned, they stared in disbelief as the flames began to catch.

All three of them jumped from the bed.

Noel was cursing as he grabbed his pants and his gun. August picked up the torch and threw it back out the broken window.

Christmas began to beat down the flames trying to spread.

A bullet zinged past August and he shoved Christmas back on the bed.

"Stay there," Noel screamed.

"The hell I will," she said jumping up. "This is my home. I'm going to help you protect it."

August stared at her in surprise and realized she had never had her own home. She wasn't going to lose what they had. She wasn't going to let Madam Leake win.

"Then get us more ammunition," August told her. "It's

downstairs in the cellar. And for God's sake, don't let them see you."

Naked, she ran out of the room, Noel turned to him. "What are you doing?"

"She needed something to do. Something that was safe and yet included her in protecting our home," August said, peeking out the window. Wondering where the sons of bitches were hiding. They were dead men.

Another bullet broke the glass and covered him and Noel with shards.

"How did they find out she was here?"

"Don't know, but obviously, someone confided in the madam and she wants Christmas back," August said.

"Or they're trying to protect the orphanage director. That man's slime and he knows his reputation will be ruined if Christmas story her told."

Christmas came running back up the stairs. "There's five of them in the front yard and two in the back."

The two men glanced at one another. August knew this couldn't be good. They were surrounded and he feared what they would do to the three of them.

"Excuse me," Christmas said. "I saw dynamite in the cellar. Would that help?"

The two men glanced at each other and smiled. When they first moved in, they had used dynamite to clear rock.

"Darling, you're a life saver."

August ran down the stairs into the cellar. He'd forgotten all about the sticks of gunpowder. This would clear the men out of the yard.

He grabbed three sticks and ran back up the stairs.

Noel grinned at him. "Let's do this."

Lighting the stick, he tossed it out the window at the two yahoos who were sneaking around the side of the house.

Kaboom!

"Damn it," one of them yelled.

The second stick was lit and they threw it out the front window of the house at the five who were waiting for them to run outside.

At the sight of the flaming stick coming toward them, five riders kicked their horses and hightailed it out of their yard.

They didn't have to throw the third stick. After the second one, all they heard were horses riding. They might've known where Christmas lived, but they were not going to take her back.

Mr. Stephens and Mrs. Leake had lost this round. But what about the next?

CHAPTER 9

August and Noel rode their horses into town, with Christmas situated on a horse between them. She had wanted to bring the wagon, so she could wear her new dress, but feared it would be ruined. Instead she wore the men's clothes that August had bought her.

No, not the image of a good married woman, but then maybe it would keep her safe. This morning, she'd d been frightened by what the unwelcomed visitors wanted – her.

Her men had their rifles on their arms and they gave the appearance more of outlaws than ranchers. This morning's early morning visit had made them hell to live with.

At first, they worried about taking her to town, then they couldn't make a decision about leaving her at home and argued over what to do next.

Even Christmas had grown weary of them fussing about the mess the bandits had left behind. But more than anything, she realized they were afraid. Afraid of something happening to her.

And now they were going to see the sheriff.

They pulled up in front of the sheriff's office and she noticed the sign saying he wasn't there was gone.

"He's back," she said with relief. She'd been afraid their trip into town today would have been for naught and they would have been endangered for no reason.

There were still groups of men hanging out on street corners and they had watched them roll into town with curious glances. Before they left, the news she was back in town would reach Madam Leake.

Noel dropped to the ground and helped her alight while August watched the street with his rifle resting casually on his arm. At a second's notice he could pull it up, aim, and fire.

Her men were not taking any chances. This morning had frightened them.

Noel took her by the arm and led her to the door and then August stepped out of the saddle, his rifle, still in his hand.

When they walked in, Seth Ingram, smiled at the men.

"Hear you fellows had a little trouble while I was gone," he said. "The madam has accused you of stealing her newest girl."

After the last few days, it didn't take much to make Christmas angry. She was tired of no one considering her feelings regarding being sold to a whorehouse.

"Not her latest willing girl. I was sold to her against my will by the director of the orphanage," she said. "And I know there are other young girls there that did not go willingly."

It was time to bring this to an end. It was time for the young girls to be rescued and the orphans to be saved.

The sheriff stopped and stared at her. "That's a mighty big accusation."

Christmas removed the cowboy hat that had her dark hair stuffed up inside.

With a sigh, she sat and her men came to stand around her. Even now, they were protecting her.

"I knew I would soon have to leave the orphanage. After all, I would be turning twenty. But I would never have gone to a whorehouse."

After what she experienced last night in her husbands' arms, she couldn't imagine doing that with strangers every day and every night.

"Why don't you tell me your side of the story and then I'll tell you what the madam said."

Of course, they had already filed a report. They would want the law to hear their version before she could file her own grievance.

With a deep breath, she told the sheriff the events of the night that she was abducted and sold to the whorehouse. Of how the director of the orphanage told her abductors to tell the madam that he should get a free sampling.

Now she understood it all. Now she knew that she wanted no part of that life.

Even now at the thought, her stomach revolted and she could not imagine sleeping with the horrid man. Of doing with him what she had done with her husbands.

"You say there are other girls there that can back up your story?"

"Oh yes. Mary is working for the madam. We didn't get a chance to speak, but when she stared at me, she shook her head. How many other girls has he done this too?"

She glanced around his office as the sheriff sat contemplating her. Suddenly the door opened and in walked a beautiful woman who had a baby in a basket in one arm and a toddler by the hand.

"Daddy," the little boy cried and ran to him. The little boy was such a cutie. The mother smiled at the sheriff. "Busy?"

"Never too busy to talk with you," he said.

"Hello," the woman said as she walked up to Christmas. "I'm Lillian Parker."

The little boy just ran to the sheriff and called him daddy and yet the sheriff's last name was Ingram.

"Christmas Rawls," she said.

Noel cleared his throat beside her.

"I'm sorry," she said. "I just got married. My name is Christmas Brooks. This is my husband Noel."

The woman glanced at the three of them. "And who are you?" she asked, glancing at August.

"August Hamilton," he said. "Nice to meet you, ma'am."

The woman smiled at the three of them. "Why do I get the feeling there is more to the three of you than what you're saying."

"Lillian," the sheriff said quietly.

"Darling, men are sometimes a little slow. She's a new bride. If this situation is what I think it is, she probably has questions we could answer."

"She's answering questions about the orphanage and the whorehouse," he said, giving the woman a pointed look.

The woman shook her head and sat down beside Christmas. "What an unusual name. Why did your parents name you Christmas?"

It was a question she often received and it had yet to be easy to tell. She would see the pity in people's eyes and it was something she had to live with.

"I was left on the orphanage's doorstep on Christmas Eve. Mrs. Griffin named me Christmas."

"What a beautiful story," Lillian said. "It was like you were a gift delivered by Santa himself."

"Santa," the little boy said.

"Yes, Santa," Lillian said, ruffling the head of her son.

"And now you're married to these two men," Lillian said just casually dropping that into the conversation.

Christmas gasped and it grew very quiet in the sheriff's office.

"Really now? I can see when two strapping young men are enamored with a woman. You're not fooling anyone. Besides, I have two husbands myself. I'm married to Will Parker and Seth Ingram."

There were more than just themselves who had multiple husbands? Relief filled Christmas and she wished she could go somewhere and speak to Lillian and ask her questions.

But there was the problem with the madam and the whorehouse.

The sheriff shook his head at his wife. "You may have just earned yourself a spanking tonight."

She grinned. "That's what I came to tell you. We've received an invite to the Thomas household. Seems they're having a small Christmas get-together. So you'll have to wait to spank me."

There was a snicker from Christmas's men and she flicked her eyes in a way that they knew she disapproved of their actions. There was no need to laugh at how this couple were handing the situation.

"Let me finish my investigation," he said.

"Sheriff, I must ask. The pastor was going to check on the children at the orphanage. I worry that they're not receiving the care they need. I worry that Mr. Stephens is only there for the money and is stealing the place blind."

The man sighed. "If I go out there today, then I need to have an arrest warrant for Mr. Stephens. First, I'm going to visit the whorehouse and ask to speak to Mary. The problem with that is I know that will alert Mr. Stephens we're investigating him."

Lillian grew stiff. "What? The orphans are not being cared for?"

"Christmas says that Mr. Stephens sold her and several other girls to the whorehouse. I need to verify their stories."

"Oh my God," Lillian said. "Just go get the children now."

That was what Christmas wanted, but she wasn't certain her men would want ten children residing in their home.

Christmas really liked this woman and if she ever got the chance, she wanted to speak to her about having two husbands. But right now was not the time.

She glanced at her men and she could see they were communicating with one another. Would they accept the orphans into their home? There was the bunkhouse, but it would still be a lot of mouths to feed and clothe.

"Sheriff, this morning, we had seven riders attack our ranch. They threw a torch in the window and if we had not been quick, would have burned us out. The madam and Mr. Stephens are going to come after us again."

It was true and Christmas feared what they would do the next time.

The sheriff frowned. "How did you stop them?"

"Dynamite," Noel said calmly. "If you arrest Mr. Stephens, we'd like to bring the orphans to our home. We'll take care of them."

Lillian jumped up and smiled at the men.

Christmas clapped her hands, her heart swelling with so much emotion. Tears welled in her eyes and she stared at her men.

"That's really nice of you, men, considering you're newly married. Do you have a place for them all to live?" the sheriff asked.

"We have a bunkhouse out on the other side of the barn. We will make it work," August said.

Crying, Christmas smiled. Her men were giving her the perfect gift at Christmas. They were letting the children she loved live with them and she knew this would be a huge adjustment for all of them.

"All we ask is our wife spend time with us," Noel said.

Through her tears, she gazed at each man. "I'm yours. I'll spend every moment I can with you."

Sometimes that might be difficult if they had a sick child, but hopefully they would understand.

The sheriff shook his head. "You don't know what you're getting yourself into. We have two little ones and they take up so much of our time."

Lillian shook her head at him. "But you still get your time with me at night and in the mornings. And when you're really good, we sneak off somewhere alone."

He grinned at her. "Because we insist."

"And I wouldn't have it any other way," the woman said with a smile that even Christmas knew promised him time later.

Christmas was in awe of the couple. Could she become that comfortable with her men? For a moment, she felt jealous of the ease of their relationship. She glanced at her men. They were the ones who initiated that the orphans stay with them. It was all she could do not to jump up and throw her arms around them.

"Thank you from the bottom of my heart," she said sniffling.

"Come on," Lillian said to her husband. "Let's go get those children. I can't stand the thought of them being there either alone or being mistreated."

Neither could Christmas.

"Honey, I can't just go in there and take them. Let me see if Judge Weiner will give me an arrest warrant. Give me ten minutes."

The sheriff walked out the door and Lillian turned to Christmas.

"Do you have everything you need? What about diapers and food?"

Stunned, she stared at Lillian.

"We have nothing. I'm used to the orphanage supplying us with everything," she said, remembering that the pantries had always been low.

"Come on, we're going shopping," Lillian said, taking her by the arm and pulling her up out of the chair.

"We don't have a wagon," August said.

"You can take mine home and I'll get in a few days," she said. "You boys watch my babies; we won't be long."

"August, go with them," Noel said. "I'll stay here. Woman, don't you get out of August's sight, do you understand me?"

"Yes, Noel," Christmas said as they hurried out the sheriff's office.

It felt so good to be buying things that the children would need. It felt so good to be under the protection of August who watched the door to the mercantile and finally told them it was time to go. He was getting nervous at the men who were walking by.

Thirty minutes later, Lillian had filled the back of her wagon with goods for them to use to feed the children.

"But how will we get the children home?" Christmas said. "They can't ride a horse."

"Come on," Lillian said, taking her by the arm again.

August ran to stay caught up with them. If something were to happen to Christmas while she was on August's watch, she knew he would be devastated. But luckily they managed to avoid the men in the streets.

They walked to the church where the pastor lived.

"Pastor, we need your help," she said when he answered her knock on the rectory house.

In fewer than fifteen minutes, the pastor had gathered enough parishioners to help them, and together they were ready to ride to the orphanage.

When they returned to the sheriff's office, Seth looked at Lillian and smiled. "Why did I know better than to let you get involved."

"We have food and three wagons to transport the children from the orphanage."

"You're not going," he told her. "Our son is hungry and I'll soon be home to eat. And it's dangerous."

With a sigh, she smiled at him. "I knew you wouldn't let me go, but I got August and Noel and Christmas enough help they can get the children to their home."

She turned and smiled at Christmas. "You're going to be a wonderful mother to these children. If you ever have any questions, contact me. I'd be happy to help you any way I can."

Christmas felt at peace and knew their home would be perfect for the children. This day would always be remembered as the day their family began.

Lillian hugged her. "Take care of this woman, gentlemen. And congratulations on your wedding and instant family."

Not sure of what they were getting into, the three of them watched as she took her son by the hand and picked up the basket where the baby lay sleeping.

"See you at home, Seth," she said with a wink before she walked out of the office.

Christmas sighed and hoped that someday she would have that confidence in herself as a wife and mother. She wanted to provide the children in the orphanage with a real family home.

CHAPTER 10

*I*t was late afternoon when the four wagons and the sheriff on horseback pulled into the yard of the orphanage.

There was no noise coming from the big old place with its faded paint, sagging roof, and porch that leaned to one side. The building needed serious repairs. The house needed a new leader.

But most of all, the children needed to be rescued.

Normally, the sound of children either playing in the yard or scampering about the house could be heard. It was quiet. Much too quiet.

The lack of laughter and children's giggles terrified Christmas.

The men glanced at one another and frowned.

"It's too quiet," she said softly to August who sat beside her on the seat of the wagon. He reached over and squeezed her hand.

"It's going to be all right. I just know it," he said softly.

The sheriff stepped down from his horse and motioned for them all to stay back. She could see he was concerned.

Where was Jennifer? Ben? And all the others?

She glanced up at the windows to see if the curtains moved, but the faded coverings just lay against the glass. No one was peeking out. Nothing was stirring in the old house.

August set the brake on the wagon and tied the reins to it. "Stay here."

She didn't want to sit here waiting for the children to come out. She wanted to run inside and find them. She wanted to comfort them and tell them that today was a blessed day. They were going home permanently with her and August and Noel.

A quick glance at Noel and she could see he was worried.

The sheriff pounded on the door. "Open up, it's the sheriff."

Nothing. No sounds came from inside.

She couldn't stand it any longer. She had to know where they were. Jumping out of the wagon, she ran around to the back of the house to see if they were outside.

"Christmas," August yelled running after her.

She knew he would be upset, but she couldn't wait another minute. What if they were hurt or injured or, God forbid, dead.

"If they're not outside then something is wrong."

"It's too dangerous. Stay here," he said as he grabbed her arm and pulled her to him.

"Let me go. I need to find them," she whimpered against his shirt.

The sheriff tried the door and it opened easily. He motioned for everyone to stay outside while he walked in.

"Hello, anyone here," he called.

It was silent.

Tears began to roll down Christmas's cheek. "Let me go. Maybe they're hiding."

The sheriff walked back outside. "No one's here."

She pulled away from August and ran inside the orphanage, crying out. "Jennifer, Ben, Sarah, it's me, Christmas. I've come to rescue you."

At first, there was silence. Then she heard a whisper. A squeak of an old wooden floorboard and suddenly she realized where they *were* hiding. She ran up the stairs, holding her pants legs up, eager to find them and see their sweet little faces.

"It's me, Christmas," she called again. "Come out."

Then she saw Jennifer peeking through the attic door, her eyes large as she ran to her. "Thank God, it's you. We've been so scared. Mr. Stephens disappeared. We've been alone."

Anger gripped her that the man had left them all alone. What if they needed help?

"Of course, that rat bastard is gone," she said. The children ran out of the attic. Laughing, she wrapped her arms around them and knew she was saving them.

Looking upward, she mouthed the words in her heart. "Thank you."

For a moment, they all were talking with excitement. "Where did you go?"

"We've missed you," Sarah said.

"There's nothing here to eat," Ben said. "All the food is gone."

If she had a gun, she'd shoot Mr. Stephens. The man had left them to starve.

"We'll talk about it later, but for now, I need you to collect all of your belongings. I'll be around to help each one of you. You're going to live with me and my husband."

"Really? You got married?" Jennifer said, staring at her. "Where are you living?"

Just then her two husbands came up the stairs and she turned and smiled at them. "Meet my husband Noel Brooks. And this man is August Hamilton. They own a ranch and we're all going to live there."

The kids jumped up and down and screamed with excitement.

"There are wagons outside for all of you to ride in," she told the happy bunch.

The kids started running to their pallets and collecting the few meager items they each owned.

"What about the babies?" she asked Jennifer.

"They were adopted right after you left. Then two days ago, Mr. Stephens disappeared. All the food is gone. I think he left us here to die."

Rage filled Christmas and it was all she could do to control her emotions. It would not be good for the children to see her anger and she did her best to hide it, but she hated Mr. Stephens for everything he'd done.

In a calming voice, she hugged Jennifer. "You did well. You took care of them."

Tears welled in the girl's eyes. "I've been so afraid. He told us not to leave the house. Honestly, I thought we were going to die."

How could a man with any kind of soul go off and leave these children with nothing to eat? Nothing.

"You're not going to die. We have a wagon loaded down

with food. As soon as we get to the ranch, I'll fix a nice big supper."

Jennifer hugged Christmas tighter and started to cry. "I've been so scared for you. You didn't come back that night."

"It was bad," Christmas said. "We'll talk later. Let's help the little ones and get out of here."

Quickly, they all helped the children pack up their things. August and Noel assisted the boys and carried their stuff to load into the wagons. When everyone's things were in the wagons, the children looked at the sad Christmas tree.

"We can't leave it, Christmas," Ben one of the youngest boys said. "We worked hard putting up that tree."

She remembered that night like it was yesterday. The night they took her away.

Noel stepped up and knelt beside the child. "What if tomorrow we go cut another tree. Would you be happy if we, as a family, went together and picked one out?"

The boy glanced at him and frowned. "What's a family?"

Christmas's heart squeezed and she realized that Noel and August were going to make them all one big family. A tear trickled down her face and she quickly swiped it away.

She must be the luckiest woman in the town of Blessing to marry such handsome men with big generous hearts.

"That's what we're going to be," Noel said. "You're going to be my son and I'm going to be your father, if you'll accept me."

The kid's eyes grew large. "You're going to adopt me?"

"If that's all right with you," Noel said.

The little boy threw his arms around Noel's neck and clung to him. "That would be the best Christmas present ever."

Christmas watched as Noel's eyes filled with tears. "Come

on, son, let's make our first Christmas together special. Let's cut down a tree from the ranch where you're going to live."

Ben nodded. "I like that idea. Is Christmas going to be our mother? You know, she always takes care of us and we've missed her."

Running to Noel's side, Christmas wrapped her arms around the two of them. "Yes, I am, Ben. Instead of all of us being orphans, we're going to create our own family."

The children started cheering.

"No more Mr. Stephens?" James asked.

"No more Mr. Stephens," Christmas said. "No more going hungry. We're going to take care of each other. You'll have chores around the ranch, but you'll have a permanent home with us."

All of the children screamed with happiness and Christmas's heart swelled with so much love.

"Let's get out of here," Sarah cried as she ran out the door. "Let's leave before he returns. He's mean and I don't ever want to see him again."

It was all Christmas could do to not loudly agree. She had even more reason to hate Mr. Stephens now.

Christmas grasped Jennifer's hand and then she took Noel's other hand. "Thank you, my husband. You've given me the perfect present for Christmas."

He smiled at her and together they all walked out the door.

Once they had the children loaded in the wagons, the sheriff came over.

"Christmas, all the money is gone. All the food is gone. He left these children here alone with nothing. Thank God you and my wife insisted we come out here today."

A sigh escaped from Christmas and she shook her head.

"I've been so worried, but I didn't think my husbands would want them. I was wrong. Bring your wife and family out to the ranch some weekend. We'll fix dinner and let the children play."

"We would love that. If you need anything, you let me know. Be careful. Mr. Stephens is still out there somewhere and Mrs. Leake would love to try to put you back in the whorehouse."

"Not a chance," Noel said. "I'll kill them both if they try to harm my wife."

"Spoken like a true husband," Seth said. "Now, I'm going home to my family. I have to apologize to my wife and tell her she was right once again."

"Tell her I said thank you for everything she did today."

Christmas smiled. She liked Lillian and couldn't wait to meet her other husband. If she and Noel and August could create that kind of family, she'd be so very lucky.

The wagons began to roll away from the orphanage and Christmas couldn't help but look back one last time. Most of her life had been spent here and while she was glad she no longer lived there, she felt blessed that together they had rescued the children.

She reached over and squeezed Noel's hand. "Thank you, my husband. Thank you."

CHAPTER 11

By the time they reached the ranch, the sun was beginning to set and even Noel felt exhausted. The parishioners who transported the children home helped unload them and then left one by one.

Each one of them would look at the two men and smile. "You have no idea what you're in for."

One man laughed. "Your honeymoon days are over. Now you have a ready-made family."

All Noel cared about was that these children were taken care of. Plus, he could see the joy on Christmas's face and knew they had made her happy. Watching his wife assign each child to a bunk and put their belongings under the bed, he could see she had done this more than once.

"Maybe we can build some shelves for each child to put his things in," August said, walking up beside Noel and watching Christmas settle the children.

"They have so very little," Noel said. "Some don't even have a change of clothes."

"I'm sure Christmas will see to it that they have everything they need," August said. "By the way, she's in trouble."

Noel frowned and turned to stare at his friend. "For what?"

"I told her to stay in the wagon and she jumped up and ran around the side of the house searching for them."

He could understand why she felt so frantic, but August had told her to stay in the wagon. She'd disobeyed them. He hated to spank her tonight, but she had to learn. What if Mr. Stephens and some of his henchmen had been waiting around the corner. They could have taken her or harmed or even killed her.

She knew too much about what was happening at the orphanage and it would be so convenient if something happened to her. These children were innocents; they had no idea what Mr. Stephens was capable of.

"We'll deal with it when we go to bed," Noel said.

Finally, everyone was unpacked and she took them by the hand and led them to the main house. The bunkhouse wasn't far; it could be connected to the house, so that everyone was sleeping in the same building under the same roof.

Especially with Mr. Stephens running loose. Hopefully he'd headed out of town, but they didn't know for certain and while he didn't want the children, he could possibly try to hurt them. Just to harm Christmas and keep her quiet.

When she opened the door to the house, they scampered in.

"Are we rich?" one little boy asked.

"No," Noel told him and quickly realized that in comparison to where the boy had lived, it probably did seem like they were wealthy.

"We're just a ranch doing our best to stay afloat," he said. "And this spring, you kids are going to learn about cattle."

"Ohhh," the boy said, his eyes widening.

Christmas smiled at the children and then gave them direction.

"While I fix supper, I want the rest of you to practice your learning."

"But it's our first night together," Ben said.

Jennifer went into the kitchen where Christmas was preparing a quick meal of eggs.

"Let me tell you a story," August said. "While Christmas and Jennifer cook us up something to eat, Noel and I will tell you about how we came to Texas."

For the next thirty minutes, they entertained them with stories of their travels to Texas and how they became good friends. How they built their ranch from nothing but a mud house into this fine home. It had taken them several years, but they were happy.

And now they had a family.

When they all gathered around the table, he was shocked to see their bright, eager, young faces staring at them.

"Tonight is our first night as a family," Noel said. "It's four days before Christmas. We have much to be thankful for."

The hunger on the children's faces was so intense that Noel couldn't hold off another moment. He said a quick blessing and Christmas gave each child a big scoop of scrambled eggs and cheese. They had biscuits and jelly and the children soon were consuming the food.

When they were finished, he could see their eyes growing drowsy. It had been a long and eventful day for all of them.

"Time for bed," he said, ready to spend time alone with his wife.

"Thank you," Ben said as he gazed at Christmas. "Today has been the best day of my life. You rescued us and gave us a family."

Tears welled in her eyes as Christmas smiled at him. "I'm glad we're all back together. But it's time for bed. Jennifer, if you would help me get them all settled, it would be great."

"Of course," she said.

"We'll do the dishes," August said, smiling at Noel.

The man shrugged. They would have to make adjustments and get a routine started. And he couldn't wait to hold Christmas in his arms again. It was their time of night and he longed to hold his sweet, beautiful wife.

Not long after, they were waiting for Christmas to return. "I hope we don't lose our wife's attention."

"You worry too much," Noel told August. "She'll make time for us or her bottom will be paddled."

The door opened and she smiled at them. "Everyone is in bed. Now I'm all yours."

"Go get undressed and be naked and waiting for us," August said.

Noel didn't really want to punish Christmas, but yet she had disobeyed. What if Mr. Stephens had been in that house? What if he'd captured her or killed her or hurt her in some way? Yes, he knew she was trying to reach the children, but her safety was the most important thing for them.

They waited a few minutes before they glanced at each other.

"It's time," August said. "And I get to spank her."

"All right," Noel said. "Don't be too harsh on her. She's a good mother and she was just worried about the children."

Noel checked to make certain the doors were locked and that the fire in the fireplace was just embers. It was a nighttime ritual that he had started years ago.

"She could have gotten hurt," August replied as they walked up the stairs.

When they opened the door, she was lying with her head on her arms, her butt raised into the air, just the way they wanted her. Did she know she was going to be punished tonight?

The men removed their clothes and as Noel stared at Christmas's ass in the air, his cock became hard as rock. And the thought of her ass turning pink made him wish he had not agreed to let August spank her.

He would love to feel his hand against her smooth flesh and the way it would jiggle whenever he spanked her.

"Across my lap, Christmas," August said. "You're going to be punished."

"For what?" she asked as she flipped over and gazed at him. "It's been a wonderful day. What did I do wrong?"

And then her face lit up as she remembered. "I was so worried about the children."

"Do you understand why you're being punished?" August asked as she lay across his lap.

"Yes, I jumped out of the wagon and ran around to the side of the house. I just needed to make certain that they weren't in the back. I was so concerned when they didn't come to the door."

Noel sighed. "And what is our one command of you."

"Obey us," she whispered. "I'm sorry, but it's been such a wonderful day."

"When you don't obey us, we worry that you could get harmed or hurt. What if Mr. Stephens and his henchmen were in the back waiting to grab you?"

Noel had to agree with August, but he so wanted to celebrate tonight. They had a family.

"But he wasn't. And we found the children," she said with a sigh.

August ran his hand across her smooth ass. "You're getting five punishment licks and a couple of swats on the pussy tonight."

August stroked her buttocks in a soothing manner that Noel knew would be a shock when the first blow came.

Splat!

The force of the blow had her body jerking, and she squirmed on August's lap trying to get comfortable.

"Count," August said.

"One," she said softly.

This spanking would make her think twice about disobeying them again.

Splat!

"Two," she said, blinking back tears.

Splat!

"Three," she moaned.

Splat!

"Four. Please no more," she cried, moving on his leg. Her butt a nice fiery red.

Splat!

Noel didn't like when she cried and he was just about to warm August not to be so hard when he gave her the final blow. Thank goodness that was over and now they could have the fun they all deserved.

"Five," she screamed. "You said you'd never hurt me. That hurts."

"You've got to obey us," Noel said as he sat beside her and pulled her into his arms. He ran his hand over her back, stroking her trying to ease her discomfort.

"For your safety, you must obey us. We're your husbands and we will protect you with our lives, but you've got to listen to us," August told her. "We need you."

"I had to know where the children were," she said, sniffling, leaning against Noel.

Noel leaned her head back and kissed away the tears on her face before he covered her mouth with his own.

Several minutes later, August laid her on her back on the bed. "Spread your legs, baby, and let me make you feel better."

At least the man knew they needed to make her feel good and he was now doing his best to give her the pleasure she deserved.

August moved between her legs and spread her wide. Noel watched as his mouth descended onto her clit, sucking it into his mouth. Her fingers gripped the sheet and she moaned.

With a sigh, he sank down on the bed and watched as August continued licking her folds.

Noel moved to the head of the bed and leaned over her. "Open your mouth, Christmas, and suck my cock."

When her sweet lips wrapped around his manhood, she licked the head of his bulbous organ, sending pleasure spiraling through him. Noel had never experienced so much satisfaction with a woman. This was their wife and he knew the feelings he felt for her were growing in his heart.

Christmas had done everything they asked her to do, and this afternoon when she'd looked at him and said thank you, his heart had swelled with so much emotion.

They made Christmas happy and he knew what they'd done was something he had to do.

Today when they realized the dire situation these children were in, there was no question about what they had to do. And now they had a family. A family they would love and cherish and protect.

He and August had both left big, warm, wonderful families behind and now they would get to experience that closeness again.

With her tongue, she swirled around the tip and he clutched the sheets as he groaned.

"Christmas, honey, I'm going to come," he said, feeling his seed building as he shoved deeper into her mouth.

With a groan, he arched his back, holding her head tightly against his crotch as his seed spilled into her mouth. Slowly he sank deeper into the bed as pulled his cock from her mouth and pulled her chest onto his body.

"Magnificent," he said softly, holding her while August continued to lick her clit.

The butt plug remained in her ass and August pulled it out, twisted it, and shoved it back in.

A moan escaped her and she opened her eyes and stared at Noel. "Can I please come?"

"Not yet," August said. "I'm not done working you over."

"August, please," she groaned as his tongue continued to tweak her clit, rubbing over the folds between her legs, stroking her and occasionally shoving his fingers inside her pussy.

For a moment, she closed her eyes and Noel turned her head toward him. "Open your eyes. I want to watch you come. See your eyes grow large and dark with passion."

A groan escaped from her. "August."

"What do you want?" he asked.

"You," she whispered. "Your cock deep inside me."

He obliged her, shoving his member in. She gritted her teeth, holding him tightly.

"Yes, baby, do that again," he groaned.

"Christmas, you're beautiful all splayed out here for us. You are the most beautiful woman and you belong to us," August said, pounding into her. "Don't ever forget that you're ours."

"I'm only yours," she gasped.

It was all Noel could do to sit beside her and watch as August shoved his cock into her. Reaching over, he leaned down and took her nipple in his mouth.

"Noel," she cried as he nipped her little bud with his teeth.

Again, August twisted the butt plug, pulling it in and out in rhythm with his cock.

A desperate moan escaped from between her lips, almost a mewl as he rocked her body with the cadence of his cock.

"You can come anytime," August told her.

Once again, Noel nipped at her nipples and that was enough to send her over the edge.

With a scream, she cried as she gripped August's cock taking him over the edge with her. With a mighty shove, he pushed into her one last time before he collapsed on top of her.

"Oh," she cried out, her gaze on Noel as she came apart.

How could life get any better than a loving wife and a

houseful of children. Noel knew that today their lives had changed forever and a peacefulness settled over him.

Now if only Mr. Stephens had left town, life could be good.

For a moment, they lay there catching their breath, floating, enjoying the glow of the experience.

"Get the next plug; she's ready," August said.

Noel slowly rose from the bed and strode over to a dresser drawer and pulled out the box that contained the wooden dowels. Quickly, he greased up the next one.

Was she ready for the next size? That one looked even larger.

"On your hands and knees, Christmas," Noel said. "Only a couple of more of these, before we can both take you."

And he couldn't wait. To feel both of them claiming her at the same time would be the ultimate in pleasure.

Slowly she rolled to her knees and Noel removed the previous plug, massaging her buttocks, teasing her rosy-red pucker with his fingers, before Noel inserting the next size.

Gazing at her semi-pink buttocks spread before him, there was nothing more enjoyable.

When it was completely in, he gave her a gentle swat to the butt.

"That ass will soon be mine," he said.

Christmas rolled over and smiled at him. "Come back to bed, Noel. I haven't felt your penis inside me tonight."

He didn't need another invitation as he crawled up on the bed and sank his cock into her sweet willing pussy.

"Oh, yes, darling, this is home," he gasped as he plunged deeper inside her. "Home sweet home."

CHAPTER 12

*A*ugust watched as Christmas helped one of the little boys with his shirt. The child was just learning to button and she patiently showed him what to do and then smiled at the child.

"Your turn," she said. "I left you three."

The boy struggled but managed to get all three of the buttons through the loops of the shirt.

"Yay, everyone Joe buttoned his shirt," she said. "I'm so proud of you."

The boy ducked his head and smiled. The other children were busy and glanced over and smiled at the child.

Noel came in from outside where the wind was blowing hard. He glanced at everyone and shook his head. "I don't know if this is going to be a good morning to go cut a tree or not. It's cold outside. It might even snow."

"Snow?" Ben said, jumping up and down. "We can build a snowman."

"Don't get excited yet. Let's wait and see what it does," he said. "If the wind stops blowing, we can get a tree this afternoon and decorate it tonight."

Jennifer took a bowl of popcorn over to the little ones. "We're going to make strings of popcorn to put on the tree. Ben and Joe, you hand me and Sarah popcorn."

Warmth filled August's chest as he glanced around. This reminded him of his family when he'd been a little boy. The memory of his brothers and sisters decorating the tree, his mother making cookies, and just the happiness that filled their home made him homesick.

But he was the outcast. Kicked out by his father for his wild ways and he had been rambunctious. Looking into the past, he regretted his actions, but there was no going back.

A little girl about four stood in front of him.

"What's your name?" she asked.

"August Hamilton," he said, smiling at her.

"Are you going to be our new daddy?"

His heart wrenched inside his chest. This morning he and Christmas and Noel had agreed that he would be Uncle August to the children. They would never understand that Christmas had two husbands and they didn't want to give the children any concern that they would ever be orphans again.

He sank down in a chair and pulled her on his lap. "I'm Uncle August. But I live here with your momma and daddy and if something ever happened to them, I would take care of all of you."

The little girl's blue eyes grew wide and she wrapped her arms around his neck. "I'm so glad. I'm Eva."

Tears welled in his eyes and his heart filled with emotion. What had these children endured? What had Christmas lived through? She'd never really talked about her time at the orphanage.

But then he had never told her about his father either. Of how when he found him in bed with not one hooker, but two, he'd kicked him out and told him never to return.

The children were bringing back his memories, both the good and the bad, and his heart ached. He'd been a young, cocky man who thought no one could live without. His father had shown him differently.

"I'm glad too," he whispered. "Eva is a very pretty name."

"Thank you," she said with a smile that would someday bring men to their knees. And he and Noel would be her father. They would have to protect her from scoundrels like himself, who had enjoyed being in trouble with women. Life had come around and he would be the father trying to protect his daughter.

A sigh escaped him as he stared at the precious little girl.

"Uncle August, are you all right?" she asked. "You look sad."

A smile crossed his face. "No, honey, I'm just remembering my own childhood. And how my momma used to help us decorate the tree."

It was true. But there were so many memories he could never tell Eva.

"Who wants to decorate Christmas cookies?" Christmas called from the kitchen.

The children jumped up from what they were doing and rushed into the kitchen.

"Where's Sarah?" she asked.

Noel and August looked around the room and counted

heads. With this many children, it was hard to keep watch on all of them.

"I'll go check the bunkhouse," David said, opening the door.

A cold wind blew in and August glanced at Noel.

"Let's help David," Noel said and August could see he felt anxious.

The two men walked out into the cold. Clouds were gathering in the distance with a rumble of thunder.

"This weather is getting bad," August said as they hurried to the bunkhouse.

Already they were discussing plans for adding onto the house to move the children into the main portion and not so far away. Funny how in just twenty-four hours their lives had changed so much.

And it was a welcome change. The chance to give these children a home filled August with warmth. They reminded him of the good times that he missed so very much.

David came running to them. "She's not in the bunkhouse."

The two men and the boy walked around the barn and the outer areas. Where could the child be?

"Do you think she's in the big house?"

"She mentioned the ducks she saw last night when we came in. Where's the pond we passed?" David said, anxious.

August saw Noel's face turn white and he started to run toward the pond they had on the edge of their property. It was a watering hole for birds and nearby animals. The deer especially enjoyed the water, but why would the girl go alone?

David and August ran after him. Surely, she wouldn't have walked from the bunkhouse to the pond alone.

When they arrived at the pond, Sarah was lying face down

in the water. August's heart skipped a beat and his chest filled with pain.

"No," Noel screamed and ran in and pulled her out. Lifting her into his arms, he carried her to the shore.

There he laid her on the ground and tried to push the water out of her lungs.

The child's face was ashen, her eyes closed. Terrified, he pushed on her stomach and lifted her legs into the air for the water to drain out of her lungs. Over and over, he did this until he noticed her chest making a jerking motion like she was trying to breath.

Suddenly she started to cough and then she puked, the pond water coming out. She began to cry and Noel pulled her close.

"You're all right," he said, his eyes filling with tears.

She coughed up more of the pond water and clung to Noel. Her little body shaking from the cold and being wet and the trauma she'd gone through.

"The ducks flew away and my bonnet blew into the pond."

The child had almost lost her life over a head covering. A stinking hat.

"Honey, don't ever go into the water alone. I'll buy you another hat, just don't go into the water."

She sniffled. "But it was my only bonnet."

"I'll buy you a dozen hats," he promised her. "Come on, let's get you out of this cold wind."

Lifting the child, Noel carried her to the house. August and David followed behind him. They had gotten lucky today.

When they reached the main house, Noel kicked the door open and said, "Bring a blanket."

Christmas came running over to the child. "What happened?"

Noel told her where they found Sarah and she gasped.

"Jennifer, put some water on to heat for hot tea," she glanced at Noel, and August watched the way she ran her hand down his cheeks. Even he could see that Noel was upset.

"August, would you put on some water to heat and bring me the bathtub. I think Sarah is going to get the first bath."

"Yes, ma'am," he said and she gave him a special smile. One that promised pleasure later. He would gladly accept that promise.

While the other children decorated cookies, Christmas gave Sarah a bath.

Noel sank onto the couch and Eva climbed up in his lap. "Can I give you a hug? You look sad."

It was all August could do to keep from laughing. Noel looked surprised, but then he wrapped his arms around Eva and hugged her. Tears streamed down his face.

"Thank you, I needed that," he said. "I was so scared."

"Why?"

"Because Sarah could have drowned. She could have died. Years ago, I lost my best friend. She drowned and I couldn't save her. The thought of one of you getting hurt is terrifying."

Eva nodded. "That's sad."

"Yes, it is," he said, wiping the tears away.

"We're afraid of losing you," she replied. "We've already lost one set of parents. We don't want to lose another."

Stunned, Noel stared at the little girl. August couldn't believe the wisdom from one so young.

It was amazing what they were learning from these children. They had survived the worst life had given them. And now they worried it wouldn't last. Somehow, they had to reassure them everything would be okay.

But would it? Mr. Stephens and Mrs. Leake were still out there and that petrified August.

Just then, Christmas came out of the spare bedroom where she had bathed Sarah.

"Is she all right?" Noel asked.

"She's resting. After I bathed her, she fell asleep. It's probably good for her."

Christmas went to Noel and took his hand. "How are you?"

"Terrified," he whispered.

"She's safe," she said.

"You don't understand. When I was ten, there was a little girl that I played with all the time. In fact, I had a crush on her. Sadie Jones. We were playing close to the river and she fell in. I jumped in to save her, but the current took her away and her heavy skirts were too much. She drowned before I could reach her."

Christmas pulled Noel to her. "But today you won. You saved Sarah. The water did not take her. You're a hero in her eyes and mine. Thank God you were here and knew what to do."

If only Christmas knew how close the little girl had come to drowning. If they had been moments later, he doubted that Noel could have brought her back to life.

If this was what being a parent felt like, he wasn't so certain he could do this. And yet, he could not go off and leave these children.

He needed Christmas and he needed this family. There was no way he could ever walk away.

The smell of cookies filled the house as well as the children's laughter as they iced the freshly baked cookies. Love swirled around them all. Even August. Because watching Christmas, experiencing Christmas each night, he was falling in love with her.

And that scared him.

He was the banished man. The man who had been rejected by the family because of his bad behavior.

Could he be a good man for these children? For Christmas? Just looking at his wife, he wanted to take her into his arms and smother her with kisses.

But they had a house filled with children.

Suddenly a gunshot cracked the window, the bullet hitting the wall right above Eva's head.

She screamed and he yanked her away from the wall and covered her body with his. Damn, Mr. Stephens had to ruin their day again. The man didn't want these children, but he also didn't want them to have the happiness they deserved.

"Everyone, get down," Noel cried as he shoved Christmas to the floor.

"Damn, could this day end any worse," August said.

"Uncle August, you said a bad word," Eva said, looking up at him from the floor.

That sweet innocent face melted his heart. "You're right, Eva, it was wrong of me. I'll do better."

"Good thing Mr. Stephens isn't here. He'd wash your mouth out with soap."

But August feared that Mr. Stephens was here along with his men. He'd be a dead man if he tried to put soap in his mouth.

More bullets flew through the windows, smashing the glass.

David covered the crying children in the kitchen.

"Stay down," August hollered, waiting for the deluge of bullets to end. He was going to kill the son of a bitch who did this.

They were terrifying the children. They were terrifying his family.

When all of the windows in the house were broken, the gunfire ceased.

August jumped up and stood to the side of the opening.

"Uncle August, stay down," Eva cried.

"I'm being careful. But I have to know who did this," he said as he opened the door and ran outside.

Five riders were racing away from the house. Five riders who he would track down and kill.

One man glanced back and grinned at him. August raised his rifle and fired a single shot. It hit the man in the leg and knocked him off his horse. He screamed in pain as he hit the ground and rolled. The other riders continued to ride off, leaving him behind.

August walked slowly over to the man. He rolled him over and the man screamed.

"Why did you shoot me?"

"Stupid question," August said as he kicked him in the leg.

The man screamed again.

"Who sent you?"

"No one," the man said with a gasp.

"You just enjoy riding to someone's house and shooting out all the windows?"

The man glared at him.

"There were children in the house. They were terrified. All the heat is seeping outside now."

The man tried to rise, but August pushed him down.

"Again, who sent you?"

Noel came running up. When he looked down at the man, a grin spread across his friend's face.

"Charles Bates, still getting into trouble, I see," Noel said. "I'm sure there is a warm cell in the jail waiting for you. But first, I can't go off and leave my family with holes in all these windows."

The man's face tightened with pain.

"Looks like you're hurting," August said. "It could be by the time that we get you to town, gangrene could be setting in. You could lose that leg. Was it worth it, scaring a bunch of children who don't have anything in this world?"

The man grabbed his leg. "Clean it out."

The wind blew and August knew he wouldn't be touching the man's leg.

"Sorry, but I don't keep alcohol on the ranch. You'll have to wait. And no, I'm not getting you out of the cold either. Those kids don't need an ugly face to put with the terror of what happened."

The wind blew and rain began to fall.

"Dang, and now it's going to rain."

"Come on, man, at least give me a blanket."

Fury filled August and he leaned down near the man. "Those kids are in a house that is growing colder by the minute because you and your friends decided to shoot out the windows. You're not getting any sympathy from me."

August glanced at Noel and shook his head.

"I'll go help Christmas fix the windows and then we'll take him into town."

"All right," August said though he didn't want to leave Christmas and the children alone. What if the men returned?

About twenty minutes later, Noel returned with a wagon.

"Let's load him in and I'll take him to town. You stay here with the kids," Noel said.

August didn't feel comfortable with either decision, but what could they do?

He stared at his friend. "Are you sure?"

"Yes," Noel said. "We can't leave our family here alone. Those men could attack again."

This was August's biggest fear, so he agreed with his friend, but he also worried about him.

"You be careful and get back home," he said.

"Oh, I'm coming back. My sweet wife is giving me those looks that say she needs to be fucked."

August laughed. They lifted the man and put him in the wagon.

Noel climbed up in the seat and drove away while August looked around at the empty fields before he made his way back to the house. Back to their new family.

CHAPTER 13

The trees lined the road as Noel drove the wagon toward town. This would be a good time to stop and pick up gifts for the children. He wanted their first Christmas together to be special. These children deserved their best Christmas ever.

And most of all, he wanted to get Christmas something special.

When they married, she didn't have a ring and before he returned to the ranch, he wanted to get her a wedding ring from himself and August, who he knew would agree to a band of gold for their sweet woman.

What a blessing she'd been to their lives. And he felt thankful they had saved her that night from being just another working girl.

The rain and sleet began to come down harder and he was so glad that he'd worn his water repellent duster. The weather was nasty, cold, and wet with little pellets of ice pelting him.

"Do you have to hit every damn hole in the road?" Charles

asked, thinking he didn't care if the man lived or died. He'd terrified the children and Christmas.

"Did you have to attack my ranch? Who hired you?"

The man lay back under the tarpaulin from Noel's time in the army that had tar on one side to repel the water.

It was more than the sucker deserved.

"I'm certain Sheriff Seth will be happy to see you, Charles. You seem to like visiting his jail. Free room and board, and this time, you may go to prison. That will be an interesting journey. Busting rocks to stay busy."

The man had been jailed several times for different things he'd done, including, theft and robbery.

"I'm not telling you nothing, except that your pretty wife will soon be back in the whorehouse."

Like hell, he would let them take Christmas and put her in the hellhole. That little piece of information was all he needed. Mrs. Leake would soon have a visit from him.

Oddly the original Mrs. Leake was dead, but her sister had inherited the whorehouse and she was even more ruthless than her younger sister. The woman was a heartless monster who made money off of lonely cowboys and desperate women. Some against their will.

The wagon rounded the corner and Noel saw the riders waiting in the road for him.

"Good afternoon," he called, knowing he was in trouble.

"What's in the wagon?" a man asked.

"Garbage," he told them.

The riders circled the wagon.

One of the riders slid down off his horse and walked over to the back of the wagon. He yanked the tarp back.

"Charles," he said as he glanced at Noel. "You taking him to the doctor?"

"No, he was taking me to jail," the man said, rising and sitting on the side of the wagon.

"Where's your horse," the man asked.

"Good question," Charles said as he glanced at the men surrounding the wagon.

Being outnumbered, Noel had a funny feeling this was not going to end well for him.

"Get him," the leader told the men. One grabbed the reins of the horses and one jumped in the wagon to grab his arms, while another hit him in the head.

The last thing he remembered was he wanted to buy Christmas a ring as a gift, then the darkness overtook him.

CHAPTER 14

$\mathcal{C}$hristmas glanced out the cracked glass window once again, gazing out into the darkness. Her chest tightened as she realized Noel had yet to return home.

"I thought I heard him."

"Me too," August said. The children wanted to wait to have dinner with Papa, but finally she insisted they eat. Now it was long past their bedtime and yet no one had made a move to settle them in the bunkhouse.

She feared them being so far from her and she didn't know what to do. They would be so vulnerable out in the building alone and the thought of them being there while they were under attack was too much.

"Why don't we have a sleep-over party tonight," she said. "I'll make pallets here in the living area and you all bed down here."

Poor little Sarah was running a fever and Christmas feared she might be coming down with a cold or pneumonia after her escapade in the pond. Thank God, Noel had saved her.

August laid Eva on the horsehair couch. The little girl had

fallen asleep in his arms and the big man had rocked her until she slept. Both of her husbands were showing a softer side she'd never imagined and she couldn't wait to be pregnant with their child.

They would be exceptional fathers. They had been patient and kind and loving to the children and Christmas just knew this was going to be their best Christmas yet, if Noel ever came home.

Her chest tightened with pain as she worried about him. What if he'd been attacked? What if he lay somewhere along the road even now dying?

Quickly she pushed the thoughts away. No, it couldn't happen. They had just found one another and she couldn't lose either one of her husbands.

It was dark and she hoped that he had made the decision to stay in town.

Together, she and August spread out pillows and blankets and settled the children on the floor. Here, she knew they would be safe. In the bunkhouse, she feared those men would return and they couldn't get to the children to save them.

When everyone was settled, she went upstairs and checked on Sarah. The little girl was curled on her side sound asleep.

Then she went to the bedroom. August was undressing and getting ready for bed.

"I'm worried," she said. "What if those same men attacked him on the road into town? What if he's dead?"

August wrapped his arms around her and held her.

"I'll go looking for him in the morning. Do you know how to shoot a gun?"

"No," she said.

"In the morning, I'm going to show you and David. He's

old enough that he should be taught how to shoot. Then I'm going to town to find Noel."

Christmas squeezed her hands together in prayer. She couldn't stand the thought of losing the man she loved. He brought sunshine into her life. After she'd married him, she realized how empty her life had been. Now she had so much, but she couldn't lose Noel.

Her husbands had rescued and saved her from the whorehouse. They'd made her feel so very special and now they had taken on the responsibility of caring for the other orphans. For that, she was forever grateful.

"Come on, crawl in bed and I'll hold you until you fall asleep. Tomorrow is going to be a trying day."

After she removed her clothes, she snuggled into bed beside August. The bed felt empty, like an abyss, without Noel on her other side.

August blew out the lantern and they lay there in the darkness.

"Promise me that tomorrow you'll be safe. I can't lose both of you at the same time. I can't lose one of you."

Rolling over, August's mouth covered hers, his tongue sweeping through her mouth as he nibbled at her lips. Both of her men, she realized, she had fallen in love with. Both of her men she needed by her side.

When he released her lips, he pulled her tightly against him. "Try to sleep, Christmas. The children are going to be frightened tomorrow. They're going to need you reassuring them that everything is going to be fine."

"And I'm going to need you supporting me and making me think that nothing can come between us. Nothing."

His hand stroked down her arm. "Darling, nothing can come between us. You're ours and we belong to you."

"But there are enemies who do their best to separate us."

"We won't let them," August declared. "Not even death will separate us."

With a sigh, Christmas cuddled closer to August and prayed that Noel was sleeping safely in a hotel room.

CHAPTER 15

*A*ugust was loathe to leave his family, but his friend was missing and he had to find him. He gave David and Christmas quick instructions on how to load and fire a weapon, but he didn't feel comfortable that they could protect themselves.

But he had to go in case Noel needed him. Plus, the sheriff should know they were still being attacked before August killed them one by one.

His best bet was to get to town, find Noel, and return before anything happened. Before the men revisited and attacked his family.

As he left the ranch, he glanced back one last time looking to see if he could see anyone watching him. Anyone who might want to ambush them while he was gone.

But only the cattle and the ducks on the pond witnessed him leave. Knowing he needed to get back as soon as possible, he lightly put his spurs into the side of his horse.

He rode hard to town, only slowing when he reached the edge of Blessing. His first stop was the sheriff's to make certain Noel had brought in Charles. Noel would've talked with Seth last night.

The men who had been hanging around the edge of town were no longer there. The streets had returned to normal and that concerned him. Christmas was safely tucked away at home.

Had they given up on finding her?

When he pulled up in front of the lawman's office, he slipped down and tied his horse to the hitching post. He glanced around for the wagon. Nothing.

Walking into the sheriff's office, he glanced at the jail cells. Empty. Charles was not here.

"Good morning, August, what brings you here?"

"Noel is missing," he said.

While August told him about what happened, Seth stood and strapped on his guns.

"That damn Charles Bates can't stay out of trouble," he said. "I'm hoping that soon I get enough on him that he goes to prison."

For the first time, August's chest tightened with apprehension for his friend. He'd never made it into town and Charles was not in jail. Noel was truly missing.

What had they done with his friend?

"Let's start at the hotel. Maybe he took Charles to the doctor since you said he was shot. Maybe he spent the night there."

In his heart, August knew that Noel would have returned home unless he was dead. Something was holding him back and he wanted to march straight over to the whorehouse but didn't.

First, they walked through town, then they went to the hotel and finally to the whorehouse.

The sheriff opened the door and walked in.

"Mrs. Leake," he commanded. "Get her."

The place was dark, quiet, and smelled of unwashed bodies. Most of the women were probably upstairs still sleeping off the night before. But one lady in a see-through robe came strolling down the stairs, her body on full display for him and the sheriff.

Like an advertisement on display, sheer satin covered her breasts and thighs, but he wasn't interested. He had the best woman in the world. Why would he want this one? If this was to tempt him, it wasn't working.

If anything, it repulsed him.

"Hello, gentlemen," she said. "Mrs. Leake is unavailable. She has a really bad headache." The woman leaned in closer to them. "Too much alcohol last night, I suspect."

Rage filled August, but he tried to control his emotions. Right now, he wanted to go room to room in this big old house searching for his friend.

The sheriff smiled. "That's a shame. But you tell her that if she's not down here in five minutes, I'm shutting her down."

The woman's eyes widened and she glanced between them. "Is there a problem, gentlemen?"

Like she didn't know why they were here. August could see in her eyes that she was just trying to delay them. Stalling them from finding his friend and he was about to go crazy with rage.

"Yes, my friend Noel Brooks is missing. And I'm going to find him," August said.

Leaning in close, she glanced around the room. "Something happened last night. I don't know what, but there was a big ruckus and then the riders left."

"Where did they go?"

The woman shrugged. "Don't know. They didn't tell all of us who were watching."

Just another delay tactic and it wasn't working.

"Great information, but we still need to speak to Mrs. Leake," August said, his tone not at all friendly. The woman may be able to manipulate lonely men and deprive even more money from them, but her tactics weren't working right now.

"Go get Mrs. Leake," the sheriff said.

The woman hurried back up the stairs and the two men glanced at each other.

"What did they do with Noel?" August said.

"Don't know. But I'm wondering what happened last night and why she would even mention it."

A few minutes later, the woman returned. "Follow me."

She led the two men up the stairs, down a hallway, and through a doorway. When they entered the room, it was dark. The curtains were closed and you could barely see the woman in the bed.

A big burly man stood in the corner watching them, a gun strapped to his hip.

"Mrs. Leake," the sheriff asked.

"Please lower your voice. My head is killing me."

"Where is my friend Noel Brooks?" August said, knowing that if they killed Noel, he would burn this place to the ground.

"How would I know? If he didn't come in here looking for a woman, then I don't know where he is," she said. "Who is Noel Brooks?"

August's fists tightened and he tried to swallow his rage, but right now, he just wanted to punch the stupid woman. But that would get him into all kinds of trouble.

It was just another stall tactic and he was about to run out of patience.

"He married Christmas Rawls, the girl you bought from the orphanage. The one that Mr. Stephens sold to you," the sheriff said.

A second man stood in the corner watching everyone and if it hadn't been so dark, August would have made certain he was not one of the marauders who shot out the windows of his home.

"Oh, that girl," the woman said, holding a damp cloth to her forehead. "She's been nothing but trouble."

"And if I don't find my friend, I'm going to tear this house down looking for him."

The woman gave a little laugh. "Quite dramatic, Mr. Hamilton. Go ahead and look around, but you're not going to find your friend here."

The woman seemed to sink farther into the bed. She seemed so certain, that for a moment, August doubted that Noel was here. But if not here? Where?

"Do you know anything about a group of men who came to our home and shot out all the windows?"

The woman seemed to drift for a moment and then she replied. "Why would I? I was here all night long. Setting my girls up with men. Now if you'll excuse me, I'm drifting off to sleep."

It was all August could do not to start going through the house.

"James, show these gentlemen the door," she whispered.

"If I learn that Noel was here last night, your business will be shut down," the sheriff told her.

The woman sighed. "Good. Then I'll get some rest without the law being in my bedroom."

The man ushered them out the door and out of the house; the two men stood there and stared as he closed the front door on them.

A very young woman walked past them and quietly said, "Follow me."

When they reached the edge of the home, she glanced back and pulled them around the corner.

She turned to them. "Noel was here last night, but this morning they moved him to the orphanage. You need to hurry. They're planning on setting up a trap and killing all of you and taking the orphans back."

The sheriff glanced at her. "And you are?"

"I'm Mary. I used to live at the orphanage until Mr. Stephens sold me to the whorehouse."

August's breath caught in his throat. This was what they planned for Christmas and probably Jennifer next. And eventually they would work their way to Eva and he'd kill the first man who touched her.

The sheriff sighed. "We're going to leave, but when I get through, I'm coming back for you."

A tear trickled down the girl's cheek. "Just save the others, so that no other girl gets sold to Mrs. Leake. She's a brutal task master."

The woman turned and they stared at the belt marks on her back.

"She did this to you?"

"Yes," the woman whispered.

"The woman is going to be spending time in my city jail," Seth spat. "Even her sister wasn't this mean."

More tears rolled down the girl's face. "Please be careful leaving. If they know I've tipped you off, they'll kill me."

And August knew her words were true. If someone would beat someone that badly, they would think nothing of killing her.

She peeked around the side of the house. "Go."

The two men all but ran back to the sheriff's office.

"Dear God, Christmas was right. They've been selling girls to the whorehouse."

The two men climbed onto their horses. August nudged the sides of his mare and they hurried through town. They had to get to the orphanage and rescue Noel.

CHAPTER 16

Christmas heard the rider and ran to the window. She watched in horror as a man sitting on horseback drew back an arrow and it hit the front door.

Fear rippled through her body seizing her lungs.

"David, grab your gun."

Shaking, Christmas picked up the weapons and moved the cloth that they had stuffed in the holes of the window and pointed their rifles at the man. Terrified, she aimed her rifle on the rider.

She would fight to the death for the children.

He laughed when he saw them and then turned and rode away. Why would he not attack them more? Were there more riders outside and they couldn't see them.

"There is a piece of paper stuck on the door," David said, leaning out and looking at the front entrance.

What did that mean?

Christmas set the rifle down and walked to the door. "Everyone, stand back. David, you know what to do if something happens to me."

Several hours ago, they had a private conversation and she told him that if she were taken or killed, he was to stay behind and defend the children. They were the most important and she would gladly give herself over to save her husbands or her children.

"Hurry," he said.

She stepped outside and pulled the paper from the arrow. With a quick glance, she went back inside and quickly locked the shut door.

With a sigh, she glanced at the note and read it aloud.

"If you want Noel to live, come to the orphanage."

August had given her strict instructions not to leave the house. But how could she let them kill Noel? She loved him that much and had no choice but to go to his side.

The children were looking at her, some had tears in their eyes.

"Please don't go back there. That place is haunted," Jennifer said.

"Don't go," Ben said crying. "They will kill you."

Her life didn't matter at the moment, Noel's did.

With a deep breath, she smiled at them. "You know I love you all. But Noel is my husband and I must go do what I can to save him. You are all going to be brave boys and girls. Jennifer is in charge. David is going to protect you. If the bad men return, Jennifer will take you all to the attic and you're to hide there. I'm hoping to be back before dark. Uncle August should be home before dark too."

She hoped and prayed that what she was telling them was true. By now, August had been in town talking to the sheriff. Unless they had captured him as well.

"Do not leave the house for any reason. Do you understand me?"

"Yes," they said crying.

The thought terrified her. Grabbing her rain poncho, she put it over the new dress she wore for the first time. If she was going to die today, she wanted it to be in this dress.

Glancing at the little ones, her heart ached, but she had no choice but to go to Noel. They knew when they delivered her the note, she would go. She feared they were waiting for her outside the gate of the ranch.

She hurried into the room where her husbands stored their weapons and slipped a bowie knife into a pocket in her dress. With all her heart, she hoped she didn't have to use it, but it would be with her in case she needed a weapon.

And she would use it to defend her husband's life or hers.

Standing at the door, she glanced at Jennifer. "You can do this."

The girl slipped her arms around her. "I know I can, but we want you. Come back to us."

"I will," she promised, knowing there was no certainty. She could very well die today.

"Be good children. I love you," she said. "And keep the doors locked."

"Bye," they called out.

As Christmas walked out the door to head to the barn, Mr. Stephens stood waiting for her. Shock filtered through her and she knew she was already in trouble as he leveled a gun on her.

"About damn time. I feared I was going to have to come in there and take you," he said, gazing at her. "Damn, I think you're even more beautiful. Sex must agree with you."

Anger resonated through her. How dare he mention the loving act between her and her husbands.

"Why couldn't you just let things go," she said.

He laughed as he pulled a horse forward. "Get on. You're going to be working tonight on your back."

Fear spiraled through her. "No, I'm going to the orphanage. The note said come if you want to save Noel. He's my husband."

Why had the plan changed?

The man shook his head. "Women are so stupid. He *was* your husband. Now you're his widow and you owe a lot of money for all the trouble you've caused."

Stunned, the meaning of his words washed over her and she felt like someone had hit her in the chest.

With a wail, she started to cry. "No, please tell me you didn't kill him. Please."

"Honey, he's dead and probably buried by now. Let's go. You're going to spread your legs for randy cowboys tonight."

Before, she hadn't known what being sold meant. But this time she did, and she felt the knife in her pocket. She would do everything she could to save herself.

But Noel. No, not her sweet husband who had given her so much. In some ways, she felt responsible for his death. Because he'd rescued her, they had killed him. And she would do everything she could to kill the bastards who took his life.

With a glance back at the house, she gave a little prayer they would be safe until August came home and learned that she had left to rescue Noel.

A cold wind tussled her dark hair.

"Where are the other men?"

Mr. Stephens laughed. "They are long gone. I knew you

would not come out of the house for me, but you would for Noel. Too bad he's dead."

A shiver rippled through her body. No, he couldn't be dead. No, no, no.

"You won't be cold for long," the man said with a smile. "Now let's go. Kick that mare and let's get to town before night falls."

She wrapped her hand around the hidden knife's hilt. She would kill if she had to.

Mr. Stephens raised his brows. "And if you try anything stupid, I will go inside and shoot ever one of those snot-nosed yard rats in the head."

CHAPTER 17

*N*oel woke and knew he was in trouble. Tied to a chair, he could not move his feet or hands. A rope was wound around his chest, holding him in the chair.

His head was pounding and he felt nauseous.

Opening his eyes slowly, he glanced around the empty room. It was the orphanage and he knew they had set a trap.

The old house was quiet. Too quiet. Even the mice seemed to have deserted the building.

There was a bottle of what looked like nitroglycerine strapped to the door. One good kick and the house would explode and anyone near would be dead.

"Anyone here?"

No one answered him and he feared this trap was for August and the sheriff. But what about Christmas? The children?

It was one way to kill all three of them at once and then the scandal of the director of the orphanage selling young girls to the local whorehouse could be covered up.

With a new sheriff, Christmas would be forced to go to

work for the whorehouse and the director of the orphanage could continue making money on the side.

An ingenious plan that he planned on sabotaging. Today wasn't going to be the day he died if he could help it.

Yes, they would need a new orphanage, but somehow he thought the director was a good enough con artist that he could convince the people of Blessing to donate.

The image of his wife came to mind and tears swelled in his eyes. Though they had only been married days, already she had claimed his heart as hers and he couldn't die without telling her how much he loved her. How much he needed her in his life, bringing him joy and happiness. How much helping the children made him feel so proud of her and what they were doing.

He wanted years with Christmas. Years of watching the children grow, of his own baby swelling her stomach and years of the three of them living happily together.

Noel had to get loose. Somehow he had to warn the sheriff and August there was danger and they could not enter the orphanage.

He began to struggle, fearing that soon he would hear August and the sheriff ride up. The blow to his head had been hard and they probably believed he would not wake until it was too late, but sometimes plans didn't go the way you wanted. And he intended on doing everything he could to thwart their misdeeds.

They had tied him very tight and as much as he struggled, he couldn't loosen the ropes. His wrists were raw from trying to loosen the knots. Nothing.

Looking around the room, he searched for something, anything, to help him. A window stood on the other side of the room. With his knees bent, he tried to lift himself in the chair and hop across the floor. Impossible.

Knowing he had to hurry, he began to rock the chair back and forth, trying to get it to fall over, hoping and praying that it would break into a thousand pieces when it did.

It wasn't a well-made chair and only had a straw bottom. Surely it would break when it hit the floor.

Moving side to side, he finally felt the legs tip and he landed on his shoulder, but the chair didn't break. The wood held together and he sighed.

His shoulder throbbed, but that pain was nothing compared to the thought of people he cared about dying.

"Dammit," he said. Why couldn't something go his way today?

With his arms still tied behind the chair, he pushed himself across the floor, dragging the wooden chair with him. You would think the ropes would've come loose, but whoever tied them made certain they were strong.

The sound of horse hooves had him halting. Was that August and the sheriff? Or had the bad guys returned?

If they kicked in the door of the house, the nitroglycerine would go off, killing them all.

He had to get their attention, but how? He scooted the chair as close to the window as he could.

"August," he screamed. "Don't open the door." Again, he screamed. "Don't open the door."

He could hear boots on the wooden porch.

"Don't open the door."

They were standing in front of the door and he feared any moment they were all going to die.

He scooted the chair next to the wall of the window and

kicked it, though the ropes made it difficult. Over and over he hit the wall with his feet. Fearing that he would set off the explosives with the shaking of the walls.

Screaming as loudly as he could, he yelled again, "Don't open the door or we all die."

The boots walked toward the window and suddenly August was raising the glass.

"What the hell you doing down there?"

"Don't open the door," he yelled. "They put nitroglycerine there."

August turned toward someone. "Stop. If you open that door, the house will explode."

The sheriff appeared at his side and glanced in the window before he crawled in. August came in after him and they sat the chair back up and untied him.

"Damn," the sheriff said, glancing at the jar of clear liquid. "If that's nitro, we would all be dead."

"Convenient," August said. "Is there anyone else here?"

Noel sighed. "No one answered when I yelled."

When the knots came loose, Noel's hands began to sting as the blood returned. He slowly stood and began to rub his fingers. His wrists were raw from the rough hemp bindings.

"What about Christmas and the children?" he asked.

"They're at the house. I showed them how to use a gun and then I went in search of you. She's worried sick about you."

Noel nodded and closed his eyes. "This has got to end."

"Agreed," August said. "They've now endangered our children and now us. We have a family to protect. I'm done."

The sheriff came back down the stairs. "No one is here. Let's get out of here before that nitroglycerine decides to blow."

The three men crawled out the window. They found the wagon on the side of the house, still harnessed to their horses and Noel climbed onto the driver's bench.

"Take your horses and get at least a thousand yards from the house. I'm going to set off their trap. Maybe they'll hear it back in town and believe that we were all killed."

It was a good plan. The orphanage sat outside of town, but not far, because the children still attended school.

With his head aching and his shoulder pounding, Noel drove the empty wagon away from the orphanage.

When the men were far enough away, the sheriff picked up his rifle and fired a shot into the front door of the house.

Kaboom!

The house exploded, sending wood flying. The old house, which had barely been standing, collapsed, the roof rising into the air and then crashing down, smashing onto the dirt. Dust and debris billowed out before dissipating.

Noel stared at the place where the outlaws planned for him to die. He was furious. Roaring mad at how they had treated him and his family.

The time for inaction was over and everyone involved was going to know his feelings when this was all said and done.

But first, he had to get home.

The men who had taken him were confident. Too confident that they were going to win, but he had a surprise for them.

Love was on his side, but first, he had to make certain his wife was safe. Then there would be some hell raising for what they had done the last two days.

"We need to ride to the ranch and make certain that Christmas and the children are all right," Noel said.

"Agreed," August said. "They're up to something no good and I fear it has to do with our Christmas."

"Yes," Noel said. "We've got to stop them."

"I'm going with you," the sheriff said and they turned their horses and the wagon toward home.

It took them almost an hour to reach the ranch and when Christmas didn't run out to meet them, terror gripped Noel. She would have been the first out that door.

"She's not here," he said as he slid off his horse and ran up to the door, fearful of what he would find inside.

The house was quiet.

"Christmas, Jennifer, David," he called.

Then he heard the upstairs attic door open and footsteps on the stairs. They had been hiding.

Jennifer came running down the stairs first and then David and then the other children.

"Thank God, you're all right," Jennifer said.

"Where's Christmas?"

"She went to save you," Jennifer said. "She's not with you?"

"No," he said, fear cascading through his veins. It had been a trap to get her alone and out of the house.

David, still clutching the rifle, stepped in front of Jennifer. "Not long after August left, an arrow slammed into the front door with a note on it."

He grabbed the note from the kitchen table and handed it to Noel.

"If you want Noel to live, come to the orphanage," Noel read. He glanced at August. "We know she's not at the orphanage, because we blew it up."

What if she had been hidden somewhere in the house and they killed her? His chest seized with pain and then it hit him.

No, they would not kill Christmas. With them all dead, she could now work for the madam.

"She's at the whorehouse," Noel said out loud grabbing his rain slicker and more ammunition. This cat and mouse game was going to end tonight, once and for all.

The sheriff turned and started out the door.

August glanced back at the children. "Jennifer, you're doing good. We'll be back later tonight."

"Be careful," she said, tears rolling down her cheeks.

He smiled at her. "We will. David, you're doing a great job. Keep defending the home."

The boy looked so proud and confident and Noel knew he would give his life to protect these children. After today, he would be given proper training and a good education. They all deserved a chance at a good life and Noel was damn certain they would be given every opportunity.

"I will, sir. Bring her back to us safe and sound," he said, his eyes watering.

"We will," Noel answered as they all walked out and saddled up.

If one hair on Christmas's head had been injured, he'd kill the madam and all her henchmen. Mr. Stephens—that piece of sludge was a given. He was a dead man walking.

CHAPTER 18

he madam and her girls had been dressing Christmas, preparing her for the night, when she heard the boom that rattled the windowpanes. A large explosion had come from somewhere on the outskirts of town.

"What was that?"

The madam smiled at her. "That was the orphanage, your husband, his friend, and the sheriff. All taken care of with one fatal blow."

Tears welled in Christmas eyes. "No, please, I'm here. No."

"Too late," the madam said, lacing up the corset they had put her in. Squeezing her breasts up and over the top. "If you had just stayed and done your job that night, none of this would have happened. The orphanage is gone, the children will be dispensed to other places and three men are dead because of you. Don't ever think you can best me."

She grabbed Christmas by the chin and yanked her around to face her. The woman looked evil. "You're mine for the next ten years of your life, if you live that long. Tonight you're going to work hard and long to help make up what you've done. Hope you enjoy fucking."

Christmas felt defeated. The men she loved with all her heart and soul were dead. The children...she didn't know what would happen to them. Hopefully, Lillian would help them.

But if the sheriff was killed, then Lillian would be a grieving widow, just like Christmas. She went numb. The thought of Noel and August dead made her knees weak, the pain that gripped her chest was worse than anything she'd ever experienced. She loved them so much and they were dead because of her.

When putting her face in her hands, the madam slapped her on the ass. "Don't mess up your makeup. We don't have time for your tears. You're going on soon and I have just the idea for your first client."

They pulled a skimpy red dress over her head and a woman began to pull her black hair up, the curls flowing down her back. Tonight she debuted in the whorehouse, not as a virgin, but just another girl trying to make a living, paying back the debt to the house.

Right now, she didn't care what happened to her. Death would be a relief to ease the pain of her loss.

Numbly, she stood and let them finish preparing her. With a single blast, she had lost everything that mattered to her. Except the children from the orphanage and she doubted she would ever see them again.

Just twenty-four hours ago, they all thought they had a new beginning, but now, everything was lost. One night together and then everything fell apart.

Sitting on the bed, she waited. They brought her food, but

she refused to eat. They brought her liquor and she did not drink.

One of the girls looked at her. "Darling, you have to accept this way of life. You have no choice."

For a moment, she glanced at the woman and then anger rushed through her. "Like hell I'm going to accept this. I'm going to make the madam's life a living hell. That's what she did to me."

The girl sighed and shook her head. "She'll beat you until you wish you were dead."

"Right now, that's what I want. To die," she said. But then she thought about the children and knew for them she had to try. Noel and August would want her to keep living for them, when all she wanted was to be with her husbands again.

Even if it were in heaven.

The memory of their handsome faces brought tears to her eyes. She had not even had time to cry and mourn for them because tonight she was the main attraction once again.

"It's time," the madam said, glancing at her. "And if you give me any trouble tonight, I'll beat that white ass of yours until it bleeds. Do you understand me?"

Christmas glared at her. "You had my husbands killed. All I can say is you better have one eye open at night when you sleep. Because I'm coming for you."

The woman gasped and walked away.

One of the ladies whispered to her, "Oh, honey, I don't think that was a good thing to say to her. She's mean as a rattlesnake. Probably more poisonous too. She'll give you the worst clients. The ones that will make your life hell."

The woman had taken everything from Christmas and no

longer would she lie down and play the victim. It was time to fight.

"If she killed someone you loved, how would you take it?"

The woman nodded. "Just be careful; she's a mean bitch. I thought her sister was bad, but she's even meaner."

The madam walked onto the stage and she glanced back at Christmas, an evil smirk on her face.

"Back tonight is Christmas. Once again, she's up for auction, but not for her virginity. Tonight, she's looking for a man who likes to play mean. Someone who will whip her with a bull whip and then take her in the ass. Make her your slave girl for the night. Make her crawl and beg you to fuck her."

Christmas gasped. So this was how she would get even with her. By selling her to some sadistic man who wanted to hurt her.

The bidding started and all the defiance she felt drained from her at the thought of what a man might do to her.

"Oh no, there's going to be trouble," the girl beside her said. "Look out in the audience."

The sheriff walked into the room. He smiled at the madam. Three of the men who had shot at her home started walking quietly to the back. She could see they were moving toward the back door away from the sheriff.

"Like hell," she said beneath her breath.

A whip, the very one that the madam was going to have a man use on her, lay on a nearby bench. Christmas picked it up and snapped it on the floor.

The madam glanced toward her, her eyes widening.

She knew she wasn't good with a lash, but she could probably do a lot of damage. Snapping it towards one man trying to get away, she hit him on his back.

"Son of a bitch," he screamed.

"Don't move unless you want another one," she said. "Sheriff, this is one of them."

The madam glared at her and stomped off stage. "Christmas, what are you doing?"

"I'm helping the sheriff," she said. "I think he's here to shut you down."

The woman's brows rose and she shook her head. "You're supposed to be dead," she said to the sheriff as he joined them.

The man grinned. "I'm very much alive, Mrs. Leake, no thanks to you. And yes, I'm here to shut your business down. You're being closed for illegal trafficking of women, attempted murder, and I know you're going to look great behind bars."

The woman turned to run and Christmas snapped the whip. The first attempt landed near the madam. The second strike caught her on the legs, creating a deep red welp.

She screamed in pain and dropped to the floor.

Men in the audience watched with stunned expressions.

It was then she saw her husband.

A scream ripped from her throat. "Noel."

She ran to him, the whip still in her hands. He had a pistol drawn.

Just before she reached him, Mr. Stephens stepped from the side and grabbed her by the back of her dress. "Don't move or I will shoot her."

She felt his gun at her back as he stood beside her, and for a moment, she was scared but then raised the bullwhip and snapped it between his legs.

The man screamed in pain, dropping to his knees, and Noel and August jumped him, pushing the evil man away from Christmas. August held the bastard's arms behind him while Noel used his face for a punching bag. Finally, the sheriff came up behind them.

"That's enough, boys. Let the law do its job." He handcuffed the man and pushed him onto the floor.

"There's a place in hell for men like you," he told the man.

"Where's August," she said, looking around in the darkness.

"Darling, I'm right behind you and, sweetie, you look mighty fine in that outfit making these assholes behave."

She turned and threw herself in his arms. "Oh, my God, I've been so afraid I'd lost both of you. Thank God."

Clinging to him, she was so relieved that both of her men were still alive.

"Let's capture the rest of these men and get them all behind bars. Then we're going to ride for home and have a hell of a celebration."

She wiped the tears that had spilled from her eyes and looked around. "That man over there. He was with them when they brought me into town."

August glanced at the man. "We can do this the hard way or the easy way, which do you prefer?"

The man shrugged and August punched him in the face, whirled him around and began to tie his wrists together.

"Anyone else?"

"Oh yes, the man that is lying on the floor, moaning. I hit him with the whip."

August grinned at her. "Darling, you make me so damn proud. I'll get him."

At this point, the men who had come to the whorehouse to drink and rent a woman hurried out the door. They didn't want to get caught up in any kind of fracas going on.

When they were all finished, there were eight men arrested for attempted murder. Mr. Stephens and Mrs. Leake for attempted murder and trafficking.

The sheriff and his deputies hauled them off to jail.

Christmas breathed a sigh of relief. It was over and she couldn't wait to get home, change clothes, and say hello to the children.

The women glanced around at the empty whorehouse. "What do we do now?"

As they began to talk amongst themselves, Mary came up to Christmas. "Thank you. I'm so glad you saved us."

"I'm just sorry I didn't find you sooner or realize what was happening," Christmas said.

She sighed. "You know, every so often I would dream about escaping, but then I didn't think I could get away. Now, I'm going to start over. I think I'm going to become a mail-order bride. Start over somewhere no one knows who I am."

Christmas reached out and hugged her. "I think that's a wonderful idea. Before you go, why don't you come out and celebrate Christmas with me and the children. Come have Christmas lunch with us."

The girl looked hopeful. "Are you sure?"

"Of course, I'm sure. We're going to eat at noon on Christmas day. I'll have one of the men to come get you."

She hugged Christmas. "Thank you. I would like to see the children again before I leave."

Noel walked up to her and she went into his arms. "Darling, it's time to go. Our work here is done."

She reached up and kissed him, not caring who saw her. "Mr. Brooks, I can't wait to get home. But first, can we wake up the mercantile owner and do a little shopping. I want to get the children a little something from Santa."

He grinned and reached down and kissed her on the lips. "You know I can't say no to you."

"Bye, Mary. We'll see you Christmas morning."

She took both of her men by the arm and they walked out of the defunct whorehouse.

When they reached the mercantile, the store was closed, but they pounded on the door. Mr. Bailey finally opened and gazed at them suspiciously when he saw her dress.

"You'll read all about it in the newspaper this week," Christmas told him. "But would you mind letting us buy some gifts for the orphan children?"

The man smiled. "Of course not. Come on in."

It took them fewer than thirty minutes, and she purchased each child clothing and a small piece of candy. And she even managed to hide a couple of things for her men.

It was going to be a great Christmas and she couldn't wait to get home.

Two hours later, when they walked in the door, the children surrounded her and she clasped each one to her in her scantily clad dress.

"That's an ugly dress," Ben told her.

"I know," she said. "And you will never see me in it again."

Her husbands exchanged a look and she grinned at them.

"Are you all right?" Sarah asked her. "They didn't hurt you?"

"No, Noel and August saved me. They didn't hurt me and those men will never bother us again. All of them are in jail."

141

The children squealed with happiness.

"It's been a long traumatic day. Tomorrow we're going to go cut a Christmas tree and decorate it. So everyone needs to get a good night's sleep."

David glanced at the men and then at her. "It's safe for us to sleep in the bunkhouse?"

"Yes," Christmas said, knowing they would trust her. Besides, she wanted them in the bunkhouse tonight, so that she didn't have to worry about them overhearing her enjoying her husbands.

"All the men are locked up," Noel told him. "This spring, we're going to add onto the main house so we'll be together."

The boy grinned. "That's a good idea."

"Come on and I'll tuck you in," Christmas said.

"I'll help," Jennifer replied as they all shuffled out the door to the bunkhouse.

Christmas glanced at her men and knew they would be waiting for her. While the children needed her attention, she needed to feel her husbands' hands on her and to tell them how much she loved them. They were her everything.

CHAPTER 19

When Christmas came up the stairs, she was exhausted, but there would be no rest. Tonight, she wanted her men's arms around her. To tell them that she loved them.

They had brought so much joy and happiness into her life that she almost ran up the stairs, eager to get to them.

When she walked in the door, they were lying on the bed, naked, waiting for her.

"Strip," August told. "Nice and slow. That dress has teased and tantalized me all night long."

"Save the dress and wear it just for us," Noel told her. "It makes all your curves stand out and teases us with glimpses of bare leg. But don't wear it around anyone else. It's just for us."

A smile crossed her face and she slowly peeled the satin down her shoulders and slipped her arms through, though her breasts were still covered.

"Oh, darling," August said.

She turned her back to them, leaned over and peeled the

stockings from her legs. The bottom hem slipped up to almost her waist.

The madam had not touched the butt plug. Slowly she bent over and spread her butt cheeks to reveal that it was still right where they had placed it.

"Damn," Noel said. "She's still wearing our butt plug. Tonight is the night."

A little scurry of uneasiness rippled through her. Tonight?

"It's time to claim her between us," August said. "Make certain she knows she's ours and only ours."

Oh, she knew that with all her heart. Last night and today had shown her that these two fine men were her husbands and she loved them.

No one could ever take their place.

She stood, whirled around, and removed the dress. Then the corset, she peeled from her body.

"Burn that thing," Noel said. "You don't need it."

A smile spread across her face. She hated the contraption and though it made her breasts bigger, her men didn't need that. They knew the size of her breasts from touching her.

The men gazed at her like they wanted to eat her alive. And she wanted them. God, how she wanted them.

"There is one little thing we need to discuss," August said. "You disobeyed me."

It was true, but she would do it again.

"You're right, I did," she said. "But no one threatens my husband's life without me doing everything in my power to save him. I promise you this. Next time, I will know how to shoot and defend myself. In fact, I think all of the children need to learn how to use a weapon of some kind. We don't want to be victims ever again."

August smiled at her. "All right. You only get lighter licks. But don't disobey again."

Christmas lifted her chin. "I'll obey you. But I'm never going to let anyone threaten my family again."

Noel smiled at her. "I think the mamma bear has spoken."

Noel walked over to the dresser where he selected a larger plug from the wooden box and a jar of ointment. "This is the last plug. I want to see you work this into your ass. Afterward, August is going to spank you and you are not allowed to come."

She lay on her back across the bed and removed the smaller one. Pursing her lips, she glanced between them and then took the plug. Noel handed her the lube and watched as she greased up the end. She placed the object between her legs but paused.

"I'm nervous about tonight, but I want to experience you both together. Both of you belong to me."

"Darling, we'll make it good for you," Noel promised.

Slowly, she inched the plug in, breathing deeply pushing and pulling. She bit her lip as the fake cock popped into place. For a moment, she simply breathed as her body adjusted to the new, larger size. There were no other plugs, this was the end, and tonight she would experience both of her husbands at the same time.

Now they could finally claim her as theirs and she couldn't wait. She could feel the wooden dowel stretching and filling her.

Just the feel of it had her breathing heavier as she gazed at her men wishing they would touch her. Wanting the feel of their hands on her body.

"Bend over, darling, and let us give you your licks, and I promise to make you feel so good afterward."

Christmas dangled across August's lap. No, she didn't like the fact they were spanking her, but she got the feeling it wouldn't be hard and it might even be pleasurable.

"Count with me," August said as he raised his hand and connected his palm with her rounded cheeks.

Smack!

Noel gripped her breasts in his hands, massaging and twisting her nipples. Explosions of desire were coming from so many places on her body that she moaned.

"August," she cried out, her hands searching for something to grip onto.

Smack, he paddled her again and again in rapid succession.

Another moan escaped.

To change the rhythm, he spanked her first rapidly and then slowly and methodically, taking care to make certain that her entire ass went from white to a blushing pink.

Noel stood to the side and began to stroke his long, hard cock. Rubbing the bead of come that spilled from the end, Christmas watched mesmerized.

Then Noel slapped her pussy and fire shot straight from between her legs all the way up into her center.

"Noel," she gasped.

"That's the kind of spanking I like to give. One that makes you moan. Up on your knees, darling. I'm going to fuck you like you've never been fucked before."

She tilted her dark curls in one direction. "Yes, I want you so badly."

Noel slapped her pussy again, his fingers lingering on her

clit, the heat filling her. Oh how she wanted them both in her, fucking her.

Both men were different and yet she knew each man just from their smell, their touch, and the way they aroused her. Each man was different, but they were her men and she wanted no one else.

Noel was rougher, but more emotional and caring. August was a little colder, but he was gentler with her, except for spanking her. He liked to spank her and she liked it too, except when he punished her.

"Tonight, we're going to claim you, together. I'll take your pussy and Noel your ass," August said.

The anticipation of both of them claiming her had her pussy throbbing.

Noel swatted her ass, sending ripples up through the plug and tingles through her body. She gasped and turned her gaze on him.

He leaned down and kissed her on the ass, running his tongue along the seam of her cheeks. "No one messes with our woman and you're ours. Do you understand?"

"Yes," she whispered. "Make me yours."

This was what she needed. What she wanted – her two men to show her they cared.

August gripped her breasts, massaging and twisting her nipples.

Noel slid his fingers over her folds before he plunged them inside her. When he pulled them out, they could see the wetness. "She's dripping."

"Please, let me come," she gasped.

Sliding beneath her, August moved until she lay on top of him, his cock nestled between her legs.

"Do you still want to come?"

A smile spread across her face. "Yes. I need both of you. Make me yours."

"Yes, you are," Noel said. "And we can't wait to fuck you."

Her ass was warm and ached, but beneath the pain was pleasure that rode her hard. Lying on the bed, she was anxious, and her body ached for her men to fill her. Never in a million years had she dreamed that pleasure could come from pain, and she liked that her men took charge of her and were rough and domineering.

Just the way she liked it. They liked to show her that they were in charge, but she knew all it would take was for her to spread her legs and they would be there.

Never had she thought that two men would satisfy her in ways she never imagined.

While she trembled with anticipation, she couldn't wait to feel them deep inside her at the same time.

Noel rubbed lube over his long hard cock.

August's fingers tweaked her nipples, his big piercing blue eyes gazed into hers. "Are you ready?"

"Yes," she whispered.

"Ride me," August demanded.

Gladly, she raised herself until her hands rested on his chest. Leaning on him, she realized the strength of August. All man. Powerful and seductive. Her man.

The bed shifted and Noel climbed behind her. His tongue caressed her cheeks as she hovered over his partner's dick. Licking his way down, he flicked her clit before he sucked it into his mouth. A groan escaped her and she pushed back, needing more of his tongue, but he pushed her toward August's cock.

"I need your pussy gripping me when I bury my cock deep inside you," August whispered. "I need to fill you up completely."

Just the words made her want to slide his cock deep inside her.

She moved above August and then slid down over his hard cock, piercing her eager, wet pussy. At the feel of him, she leaned back as she went lower and lower until she hit his pelvis. The feel of his long, hard cock snug in her pussy was almost enough to send her over the edge. The plug in her ass was tight against him.

All the pleasure from before returned like a stampede battering her with greedy lust. She gasped. Filled with cock and the plug, she was so full, so tight, and yet she wanted more.

She wanted Noel.

She moved up and down on August rigid member, rubbing her clit, needing to ride the pleasure building inside her.

Noel's hand caressed her buttocks, his hand rubbing her ass, pressing her toward August.

August gripped her face and kissed her. A moan escaped her as their tongues tangled, and still, she wanted more.

She wanted both of her men. Inside her now. After the last day, she needed them.

Noel teased her with the butt plug, pulling and shoving, stretching her that last little bit. Though it felt unnatural at first, now she couldn't wait to experience his meaty cock inside her ass. With both of them inside her at the same time, she would be so full and stretched.

A moan escaped her as he pulled the plug from her ass with one hand while the other one fondled her clit. When the plug came free, she felt like she was opened wide, empty and bereft.

"Noel, fuck me."

Leaning over, she felt the flared head of Noel's hard cock press against her trained ass. Slick and hot, the pressure of his invasion grew. Slowly he pushed his rock-hard cock into her, her muscles quivered with submission as he filled her, stretching her.

"Relax, honey. Let me in," Noel told her.

She took a deep breath and slowly released it, willing her body to stretch and accommodate Noel's cock.

He was big and she had to breathe through her nose and relax to accommodate him in her ass. She'd never felt anything so tense, so exhilarating, and so passionate.

With both of them in her body, she felt like there was no room. And yet, her body surrendered, the tight ring of muscle giving way as his cock slid deeply inside her. When he was completely in, he paused letting her adjust to the feel of him.

Both of her husbands were now inside her body, and she was completely filled.

"Squeeze me, Christmas," Noel gasped.

When she clenched her muscles, she felt as if she were attacking and holding hostage both men. Both of their cocks stuffed inside her.

Taking a breath, she moaned as Noel moved in farther, then retreated, the feel of him hard and thick and so wonderful.

A hot rush of desire raced through her as she accepted him into her body, loving the feel of both men. Pinned between them, she whimpered at how they controlled her completely.

They began to move, and she gasped, crying out at the rush of feelings.

First, Noel, then August, each pushing her closer and closer to the edge as they retreated and then filled her over and over. Between them, they maneuvered her body, bringing them all to the brink of pleasure.

August pounded into her with Noel retreating. In the middle of these two men was where she belonged. Here was her life. She needed the two of them to fuck her. To claim her. To make her theirs.

They were her men. Her husbands, her lovers. And she couldn't live without them.

"Please, can I come?" she cried, knowing she couldn't hold out much longer.

"Come all over my cock," Noel gasped.

"Milk my cock. Take it deep and squeeze it," August cried.

With a bright burst of light, a scream tore through her throat as she squeezed and held her men, working the seed from their bodies.

Pleasure filled her and their hot semen coated her insides. First, Noel, and then August, as they held her between them, their cocks buried deep inside her.

No barriers remained between them. They had marked her, made her theirs. And joy filled her at the thought of their life together.

Breathing heavily, they reluctantly pulled free from her, but held her between them. Slowly, they returned to normal, but she knew nothing would ever be the same. Her life with her husbands was perfect in every sense of the word.

"I love both of you," she whispered as she lay between

them. "You are my heart and my soul. You've given me so much and made me so very happy."

Noel reached out and stroked her hair. "Christmas, until I realized we might lose you, I didn't know how much I loved you. You make us very happy."

August held her tightly. "Yes, we love you. With you, we've created the family I lost. Now our holidays will be just like the ones I had in my parents' home."

She raised her head and gazed at them. "Taking a chance, I'm so glad that I'm married to both of you. I love you both. You've made my life complete."

CHAPTER 20

*C*hristmas morning. August and Noel had awakened their sweet wife with a sound fucking to begin the day. Even now, she looked sated and happy and even glowing in the firelight.

The children had awakened even earlier than normal and now they were sitting around the tree staring in wonder at their presents.

Yesterday, they had cut a small cedar tree, decorated it with popcorn strands, some strings of homemade garland, even put a paper star on top.

No, it wasn't the fancy tree of his childhood, it was better. Because this tree was decorated with love.

"This is all for us?" Sarah asked. The little girl had fully recovered from her almost drowning in the pond and even now she climbed up in Noel's lap.

"Yes, sweetie, it's for all you children," Noel said with the biggest smile August had ever seen on the man's face.

Their family was everything.

"It's our first Christmas together," August said quietly.

Now he had his own large family and he hoped and prayed that soon, they would see Christmas's belly swelling with another child. The more, the merrier.

David opened his present, tears swelling in his eyes. "My own gun?"

"It's time for you to learn. You can only use it when one of us is with you, but you're old enough," August told the boy. He had plans on taking him out later today and practicing.

The boy's mouth was quivering and he was blinking, trying to hold back his tears. "Thank you. Thank you so much."

Eva held a baby doll in her arms rocking it. "A baby doll. Oh, I've wanted my own baby doll for so long. Will you help me make some clothes for it?"

"Yes," Christmas said with a smile.

Jennifer held up a store-bought dress and twirled around the room in it. "It's so pretty. Thank you."

August sat there enjoying the happy sounds of the children as they opened their presents. No, the young ones had not received a lot, but to them this seemed so extravagant. He doubted they had ever had a Christmas like this before.

He glanced at his wife, Christmas. She had put the wedding band on her finger and gazed at it, tears streaming down her face.

"I love you," she said and he knew she meant both of them.

"Love you too," they both said.

Gazing around the room, he knew this was just the beginning – this ranch, his wife, his friend, and the children that were now theirs to raise.

This was the best Christmas ever with his new forever family. This family he knew would always welcome him with open arms. Looking at Christmas, he realized that she would make this house a home and he would never wander ever again.

THIS IS the end of the Blessing, Texas series for now. I hope you've enjoyed these couples as much as I have. Look for the new series Treasure Falls Brides.

Fleeing her past, Mary runs straight into the arms of danger.

Mary Beattle had to run. Even now, the law is searching for her. There was no time to bury her sister. No time to explain her actions. Only a chance to pack a bag and get on a stage out of town. Then she meets a matchmaker and soon finds herself as a mail-order bride. Wanting a fresh start, Mary gets the shock of a lifetime when she reaches Treasure Falls, Montana.

After a sordid beginning, Andrew Larsen and Jesse Sanders have turned their lives around. Now they own the local mine. They're wealthy, powerful men in the small town of Treasure Falls. But there are no women, so they order brides for the men in town.

What a surprise when the stage pulls in and they discover the matchmaker has outdone herself. But the woman they choose brings peril to Treasure Falls—a menace that threatens their

tenuous hold on their bride and exposes the unsavory aspect
of their pasts.

Also By Lacey Davis

Blessing, Texas Series
Loving My Cowboys
Two Cowboys' Christmas Bride
Two Cowboys One Bride
Two Cowboys Too Perfect
Two Cowboys to Protect Her
Two Cowboys Save Christmas

Bridgewater Brides World
Their Perfect Bride
Their Tempting Bride
Their Scandalous Bride

Treasure Falls Brides
Our Fugitive Bride
Our Desperate Bride
Our Wild Bride

**Want to learn about my new releases before anyone else?
Sign up for my New Book Alert and receive a
complimentary book. Blindfold Me.**

ABOUT THE AUTHOR

Lacey Davis is a pseudonym for a USA Today bestselling author who wanted to try her hand at writing sexy romance. With these novels, I hope to write sizzling romances that will leave you grabbing a fan to cool yourself off.

If you like hunky bad boy heroes who like to be in charge and strong pretty women who are willing to risk it all, then look no further. These sexy reads will get you in the mood. Come experience strong women who will tame these bad boys and leave them wanting more.

The End